Between Families and the Sky

Also by Alan Cumyn

Waiting for Li Ming
What in the World is Going On?

ALAN CUMYN
Between Families and the Sky
a novel

GOOSE LANE

This novel is a work of fiction. Names, characters, places and incidents are the product of the author's imagination and their resemblance, if any, to real-life counterparts is entirely coincidental. Sections from Part II of this novel first appeared in a different format in *The Fiddlehead* (Summer 1995).

The author wishes to gratefully acknowledge the financial assistance of the Ontario Arts Council in the preparation of this manuscript. Thanks too to the many friends and family who offered their reactions, comments, advice and support, and to Banny Belyea and Laurel Boone at Goose Lane for editorial direction. The deficiencies that remain are entirely mine. Thank you!

Book design by Julie Scriver.
Printed in Canada by Tribune Printing.
10   9   8   7   6   5   4   3   2

Canadian Cataloguing in Publication Data

Cumyn, Alan, 1960-
   Between families and the sky
   ISBN0-86492-169-1

I. Title.

PS8555.U489B48 1995   C813'.54   C95-950244-0
PR9199.3.C86B48 1995

Goose Lane Editions
469 King Street
Fredericton New Brunswick
CANADA E3B 1E5

To Suzanne, Gwen and Anna,
who are my family and my sky.

PART I
The Hole in the Kitchen Floor

ONE

The day of my father's funeral I stood in the doorway of the master bedroom and watched my mother weep. She was wearing a white slip, sitting on the bed with her long red hair tangled over her shoulders and her back to me. It is an astonishing thing to find your mother beautiful, in *that* way, at such a moment — I could not speak and I could not leave; all I seemed capable of was to watch with the silent, hawkish eyes of receding childhood.

I don't remember how the scene ended, whether she turned to me and said something or I finally crept away. In a way the scene has never ended — in a part of my mind it is etched in acid, and I can smell my mother's powder, see her round white shoulder in the mirror and how rumpled the sheets are (not made in three days — she would have the whole bed carted off, sentenced to oblivion). I can see too my father's clothes peeking out of the closet door as if waiting for him to come into the room, and taste still the air charged with the burning electricity of fear and love and anguish.

The funeral was peopled by a great many relatives I did not know from distant corners of the family. I don't remember much of what was said, who talked to me, or even where we were. I did not look at the body. Father had died of a brain aneurism in about the time it takes for an avalanche to tear down a mountainside that has stood for millions of years. But Father did not have millions of years. He was only thirty-two. My mother was thirty-eight. I was twelve and numb inside, as if large reservoirs of blood had begun turning to ice. An uncle I never saw again put his hand on my shoulder and said, "Son — it's all right for you to cry."

It might have been all right, but I didn't. I couldn't. I could barely breathe.

It was some days later that Grandfather arrived. He was a tall man, terribly straight and thin, with a nose hooked like a talon and a handshake of concrete and gripping eyes of ice-blue set deep beneath protruding brows. We were not expecting him. He stood in the doorway, the top of his forty-year-old fedora, utterly out of place in 1975, scraping the door frame, a huge black suitcase in his left hand. I had only met him once or twice before; my mother, who was going through some papers in the study, stopped in the hallway when she saw who I had let in, and stood speechless. Grandfather said, in his slight Scottish accent, "I'm only coming for a few days. In times like these family should stick together."

Mother snapped out of her stupefaction and Grandfather put his bag in the spare bedroom, and then we sat in the living room while she made tea. He sank into the sofa like a ship disappearing in the trough of a great sea, his knees jutting up like a bow. He was wearing the suit he would have worn at the funeral — all black except for the white shirt, the shoes spit polished, the white of his bony shins exposed between the tops of his socks and the cuffs of his trousers. His hair was the grey of a winter sky and shaved close to his head, his big ears jutting out like afterthoughts. My father wore a beard and Grandfather was clean-shaven, but there was an intensity of gaze, a restlessness that was my father's too.

"So, lad," he said. (I wasn't sure that he knew my name right off.) "What grade are you in now?"

"Seven," I said, and he seemed surprised, as if he expected me to be older.

"So — trigonometry," he said. "Vectors. Euclid and Archimedes. You're studying these men?"

I looked at him doubtfully.

"The square on the hypotenuse," he said, and when I still looked blank, he said, "More things have been done with the square on the hypotenuse than we can even remember."

"I think they've changed it," I said in a little voice.

"Nonsense!" he roared, and then Mother arrived with the tea and I blended into the furniture as Mother and Grandfather talked about who had been at the funeral, Grandfather nodding with each name as if checking against a long list he held in his head.

"I'm sorry I could not come for the day," he said, meaning the funeral. "I had to extricate myself from some very complicated matters. Believe me, if I could have come I would have. Philip was the most promising of my sons."

At that he stopped to sip tea from a cup that was almost lost in the expanse of his great hand, and Mother was left to bite off whatever it was she wanted to say. The most promising of Grandfather's sons, had he been in the room, would have raged out of it at that remark. Relations between the two had been sour for twelve years at least, over the matter of this marriage, and of me, I suppose. My father did not go to university, did not study engineering or law or medicine, the three options his father allowed. Instead he married an older woman and had a child almost immediately and started a roofing company that did well even as he taught himself the business. "People need roofs and roofs need fixing," was his maxim. He would talk about the business sometimes at night after finishing the books, while Mother rubbed his back and I lay awake in the other room, listening.

One of my earliest memories, I am almost ashamed to admit, is lying awake in my bed listening to the sounds of my parents' lovemaking. It would begin with the rubbing of Father's back, the easing of the knots in his shoulders (he was not gigantically tall and thin like Grandfather, but short and solid) while he talked about what had happened in the day — the near-accidents, the rotting roofing boards, the payment that had either finally arrived or was late again. The details would spill out like the overflow from a rain barrel, but after a time he would stop talking, and the two would make sounds together, and their old bed that they got from a garage sale the day after their wedding would begin to moan and gallop, only a few inches of plaster away from where I lay.

I am not sure when I realized what they were doing, but after a time it seemed I always knew. And I knew also that it was something that would never be talked about — that in the morning I would be grilled on what was coming up in school and Mother and Father would talk about bills and bringing the car in because the wheel alignment was shot again and were there requests for groceries? — and it would be as if the moans and laughter and the squeaking, thumping storm of the night before had never happened.

Of course there were nights when it did not happen, and usually the next morning the atmosphere would be sharp like a skate blade. The butter would be hard, the toast would burn, coffee would spill, and I would stay silent and disappear as soon as possible. The tension could last for days or could break quickly — but it usually had something to do with the sounds at night, unacknowledged, undiscussed. It was as if there was a great hole gaping in the kitchen floor which we learned to walk around while looking the other way.

When Father died the sounds at night changed, but the rule somehow stayed the same. The creaks and breathing turned into the sound of Mother weeping — of quiet, solitary pain every bit as elemental as the lovemaking, coming from the same wellsprings. It terrified me, and yet I remained calm, too, as before. It seemed natural to me that the most mysterious parts of life happened late at night, and you had to listen for them or you wouldn't know they were there.

That night our guest made new sounds echo through our thin walls. His snoring resembled a rush of locomotives shaking the rafters, rattling the windows, rumbling through the floor from two rooms away. Mother stayed breathlessly silent for a long time, and it was only very late, as I was almost asleep, that I heard her weeping, private and controlled, the new single bed she had bought giving no hint of the shudders it held.

In the morning my eyes were weary from a strained sleep full of half-remembered, hostile dreams, against which I had clenched my jaw so tightly it was painful to open. I was rubbing it as I went down the stairs and found Grandfather, wearing his undershirt and boxer shorts, black socks and black leather shoes, on his knees scrubbing the kitchen floor. I almost fell over him; he caught me in his huge hands and said, "Just a minute and I'll be through."

Mother came down then as well, too shocked to comment, her face looking old from sleeplessness and grief. She paused for a moment, then she shook her head and went into the bathroom, where she stayed bathing for over an hour. She said, "Thank you, Trafford, but that floor did not need cleaning, and you are a guest here. Did James get you some breakfast?"

I hadn't had a chance. Grandfather had already boiled up a huge pot of oatmeal porridge, large quantities of which he ate in a bowl the size of a washbasin, straight — with no milk or sugar added. Along with it he drank glass after glass of hot water, a breakfast that, he claimed, had kept his digestive system so regular he hadn't missed a single day in over forty years. He had been up since dawn, exercising in the living room with a pair of dumbbells that his father had given him when he was even younger than I was. They were of knobby, black, ancient iron with thick coiled springs inside for squeezing — the secret of his cement grip — and felt like they were heavy enough to break bones in your foot if you dropped them. When I tried to lift them, they reduced my arms to elastic bands and nearly tore my shoulders from their sockets.

"It takes a little practice," he said, gently, relieving me of them. "You have to build yourself up."

And so I was an easy conquest for Grandfather. That day I did not go to school — I had been off for the whole week on account of the family tragedy — but went with Grandfather to the best sporting goods store in town and bought two punching bags for the basement as well as a set of gloves. We spent hours installing them, drilling the holes and bolting the supports to the rafters. Then we stripped to the waist in the cold of the basement and he strapped the huge gloves onto my hands and began the first of many lessons.

"Don't punch with your arms. Release with your hips and let the arms carry through." And then *whap!* his fist would land on the heavy bag like the wrath of God, and I would go at it — *tap! tap! tap!* — sweating and grunting.

"Keep your guard up! Protect your jaw! Don't stand still — bob and weave. But when you punch" — *whap!* — "drive from your back foot. Do you see?"

We sparred a little, Grandfather holding out his huge hands for me to flail, every so often slipping inside my guard to tap my cheek and send me reeling backwards. And then he played a tattoo on the little bag, his head moving from side to side to avoid the rebound. "This is for rhythm, for speed," he said, puffing slightly. "For counter-punching.

When you see that bag coming at you, you strike and keep striking. Understand?"

I nodded gamely and got hit on the nose on the very first punch with such surprising force that tears welled up.

"Keep going!" he said. "A round is three minutes. Protect yourself! Counter-strike!" And so I hit again and again, and got hit, and kept hitting, and soon I couldn't see for the tears but slogged on, Grandfather holding up his watch to count out the seconds, the bag rattling furiously with every blow, hitting me now on the jaw, now on the side of the face, again on the nose. Finally he called "Time!" and I collapsed on the floor. I wanted to get up again, to start another round, to show him, but I couldn't stop crying. It flooded out of me, a huge release I didn't even know I was holding.

"I taught your father from an early age," he said, kneeling beside me. "He became a very strong puncher, but he wasn't as quick as you. You're going to strike like lightning when I teach you."

I nodded, wiping away the tears with my glove, and then the next tears that had replaced them, and the next. It was just the phrase that he used — *strike like lightning*. Father had used it all the time, and now I knew where it came from.

And then my Mother came down the stairs and stood with her hands on her hips, watching us. She was suddenly a foreign presence, the Other. She stood a long time silently debating, it seemed, which sharp words to use. We are a tableau still in my memory, but somehow I see us from where she was standing, Grandfather and the two bags and the huge gloves, and me huddled nearly naked on the cold cement floor. There must have been a hundred things she wanted to say, but what came out was a single, sharp, neutral word — "*Dinner!*" She turned and her heels rapped up the stairs, and my tears were shut off as if by a tap while Grandfather unlaced the gloves and wiped my face with a rag like a cornerman.

"A boy needs to know how to defend himself," Grandfather said later at the table. We had washed up and changed and his eyes were softening, trying to win her over as well. She would not look at him but concentrated on serving the potatoes and beans and meatloaf, the large spoons knocking loudly against the china. "I'm surprised Philip had done nothing about it to date." And then, "I can take the bags down if you like."

"James plays hockey," she said. She passed out the plates. "There's no gravy, I'm sorry," she said. "I couldn't be bothered."

"This looks wonderful," he said, and kicked my ankle until I said, "Yes, it's good, Mom!" There was a very long silence as we ate, the clatter of knives and forks echoing against the lack of conversation with the volume of automobile collisions. Finally Mother said, "I'm going back to work on Monday. How long do you plan on staying, Trafford?"

"What sort of work?" Grandfather asked.

"I'm a legal secretary," she said. "I'm not asking you to leave. It's just I'm sure that you have pressing matters at home."

"Nothing so pressing," he said, chewing his food.

"Well . . . I'm glad," she said, too politely. "I'm just sorry Philip isn't here. You two would have had a lot to talk about."

Grandfather kept his eyes on his plate, elaborately sticking bean after bean on his fork as if that were the most important thing in the world.

"I tried," he began.

"Bullshit you tried!" Mother said, and then, "Excuse me, James," and then, turning back to Grandfather, "We've been a family for twelve years and about the only time you ever show your face is after the goddamn funeral. Well, it's just not good enough, Trafford! It's not. Philip was so proud of us, and —" She banged her napkin on the table and rose. "Excuse me, I'm not hungry." She rushed upstairs and slammed the door to her bedroom.

Grandfather sat, his fork suspended, his mouth open. Nobody spoke that way in our house, ever. Surely the walls would collapse, the floor would buckle, the windows shatter with her words. But nothing happened. Grandfather ate his beans, then finished the rest of his plate, as I did mine. We cleared up the dishes — he washed, I dried — and Mother's plate was put in the oven to stay warm. Together we went into the guest room where Grandfather took his violin out of his huge black suitcase and played a series of haunting melodies that are not quite in my head anymore — rather they are in my blood.

Quite a long time later I heard Mother come down the stairs, open the oven door and pause. Finally she came in and sat on the edge of the bed with her plate on her knees while Grandfather played with his foot up on a chair, his eyes closed, his body swaying, one song merging into another.

And so Grandfather stayed. I don't remember talking about it at the time. The story must have come out later, but at some point I simply knew that there had been a financial collapse, that a business he had invested in had taken everything. Perhaps he never told us outright — it seemed instead we came to know slowly over the next several days as he scrubbed the kitchen floor, scraped and painted the garage, mended the fence, washed and waxed and polished the car, cleaned out the basement, clipped the hedge, turned over the garden, mowed the lawn — took care of the thousand things that Father and Mother were always too tired to do and I never thought of. He was an efficient, tight-lipped tower of household maintenance, a beacon of the work ethic from early in the morning until after he had cleared up the evening dishes, when he would bring out his violin again and play. I don't remember him adequately explaining why he was there or why he had never connected with his son in twelve years. I just remember us carrying on, as if walking around another hole that didn't need to be mentioned.

One night I was lying awake in the darkness, remembering the times my father had brought me with him to go and look at roofs, to climb the ladders and crawl across the eaves, and how he would squat on the steepest ledges, unconcerned, noting the frayed edges, the drooping slopes, the crumbling chimneys and rusting vents. He liked to look at the world from up there, from over the tops of the trees. He said it made him feel like a tall man.

I was in the middle of that half-dream, half-memory, when I heard a cry. It was Mother and she was frantic. I raced from my bed, breaking the code, forgetting the hole, stepping right into it. She was in her nightdress, almost naked to my eyes because I normally saw her in her thick robe. Her hair was askew and tears flooded down her face and the sinews in her neck stood out in thick cords. "What is it — what?" I asked. "What's happened?"

She could barely speak. She was on her new bed, ripping out the sheets, pulling the pillows from their cases, thrashing the covers back and forth in apparent madness.

"I've lost my ring!" she wailed, showing me her empty finger and then turning back to the search. "It fell off! I was fiddling and it just fell off and now it's gone! I think it's down the vent — there's no other place — oh God!" She was tearing at her hair and her shoulders were white and exposed. I had never seen her like this before, so wounded and out of control. I knelt with her and pulled the bed back and checked in the corner where the metal vent was folded with dust. It would take a screwdriver to pull it open, but I knew if it had swallowed the ring there was no hope.

"It's just, it was there and then in a second it fell off — it was just, it was there! James, find it for me, please, it's all I have, please, it can't be gone, it can't!"

And then Grandfather came in wearing his undershirt, boxer shorts and black socks, his legs long and white and knobbly. He picked my mother right up off the bed — and she is not a small woman — and held her in his arms like a baby until she stopped shaking. He didn't say anything, but put her down finally in a soft chair by the dresser, and then he and I slowly went through all the bedding and searched between the mattress and the boxspring and along the edges of the wall and behind the curtains. Then he sent me down to the basement to get a screwdriver, but by the time I returned he had found the ring — between a corner of the carpet and the moulding, obscured beneath a ball of dust.

Afterwards, when we had reassembled the bed and Mother's wedding ring was back in place, we lingered for a while. Mother could not stop crying so we sat together, Grandfather's big arms around us, and slowly he began to tell us stories about his youth, only little corners of which have stuck with me. I can't remember how many brothers he had, or why he left Scotland, or where he went or exactly when. What became clear was that for this man who had been so hard he had barely spoken to his son in twelve years — for this man, family was the most important thing, the strongest, what endured.

One scene stays with me — of Grandfather as a young man climbing the cliffs and roaming the paths that wind far above the cold North Sea, his heart in tatters over a young woman named Colleen with red, red hair and intelligent eyes that had a way of gazing far too long. On one of the craggy rest points he met a grizzled wanderer whose shoulders stooped and whose laugh was a little wild. The old man sat down with the young and offered wine, which he poured into a canvas cup, and, without asking what was wrong, the old man simply said, "We'll sit here for a time, and I will talk, and then you can talk, and I will talk again."

Grandfather talked us both to sleep. When I woke up I was in my proper bed, and when I went downstairs he was on his knees, scrubbing our old kitchen floor.

TWO

When Grandfather was twenty he nearly fell off a cliff out of love for Colleen. He was walking with her in the hills along the coast near the family village north of Aberdeen. Though it was August, the winds howling in off the North Sea were bringing squalls of freezing rain, but Grandfather's heart burned with love for the young woman some yards ahead of him. What had begun as a stroll, a "courting walk," turned into something of a cross-country race, with Grandfather falling behind despite his long legs. She was too nimble and hardly lost her breath, although she was talking all the time they were leaning into the wind, oblivion below them in the rocks and grey-white seas.

Grandfather kept after her doggedly, grimly, intent on

marrying her if he could ever get a word in. Then about an hour into their walk he simply lost track — she turned to say something to him, the sun came out for a quivering moment and caught in her eyes, she smiled in her blazing way, and he went right over the edge.

"Trafford!" she said, as he pulled himself up, death swirling a hundred feet below. "Mind your way!"

I'm not sure when I realized that Grandfather was in love with my mother. The first clues were difficult to decipher and I wasn't looking for them, and then it was too late. In his early, undeclared campaign to be allowed to stay with us he quietly "made himself useful," as he would say, bringing a lifetime's worth of marine engineering organization to bear on the tasks that keep a household running. His cooking was another matter. In the beginning, every dinner he prepared for us was a variation on leathery liver, rocklike potatoes, and greasy fried onions. He insisted that Mother should not have to bother ever cooking a meal again, now that she had gone back to work, but not even the hunger of several days could make those dinners palatable.

He was a proud, stiff and sensitive man, so Mother had to be careful how she handled the matter. She kept me from telling him how awful the dinners were — and I would have, given half a chance — and instead began giving him a few hints: leaving recipes out on the counter, bringing home some new vegetables, asking him about a certain kind of sauce. And slowly — nothing was said, there was no formal statement or agreement — they were preparing the dinner together. "Oh, look, Trafford," she would say. "I've always wanted to cook Chinese food. I got this from the library, but I don't know."

"Can't be too difficult," he would say, taking the book. "Just follow the instructions. But I haven't my glasses. Why don't you read and I'll chop?"

And so they would be an hour together in the kitchen. Grandfather could have easily found his glasses, and after a while he didn't need Mother's help with the cooking either. But they kept up the pretence and fell into a routine. Mother would tell him about her office and the cases they were handling — mostly mortgages and marriages — and the shifting tides of romance for the lawyers and the "legals" (which is what she called herself and the other secretaries) and occasionally the clients, professionalism notwithstanding. She seemed to have the confidence of nearly everyone in the office and so knew far more details than she had a right, but the grieving process had placed her for now safely in the stands as an observer. This was my perpetual status anyway, as a somewhat introverted only child with an ability to sit very still in the living room pretending to read a book while listening in on everything that was being said in the next room.

Grandfather would talk about Colleen, the magical Colleen, who never took him seriously and yet allowed him to hang around like a favourite pet, an earnest, kiddable, loyal dog who would fetch whatever you threw and was always game for a walk whatever the weather. Over the years just what they had to say to one another was washed away with the rain and tides, but what he remembered most was the special skewing of time that comes with love — how an afternoon passes like a bare half hour, and the quick stroll before sunset turns into twelve miles by midnight with the stars poking through the black and the moonlight dancing almost warmly on the ocean. She was so full of life, my grandfather's Colleen, that what remained of those long conversations a half-century later filled our kitchen with warmth and light and laughter.

Either that, or something else quite like it was being re-kindled.

"Ay, your mother's a special woman," Grandfather said to me, in the basement, as we were doing our "training" with the punching bags. "Look — keep your guard up. Never reach so far that you fall off balance. The short punch is the one that does the job." I punched some more, dancing around the big bag that barely puffed when I hit it and shuddered the whole house when Grandfather took a turn. "I knew it as soon as I met her. The first time I saw her, I said to myself — 'now there's a fine version of a woman.' Don't go telling your mother that I said that."

I nodded and hit the bag another flurry. "Then why didn't you come to visit us more?" I asked, panting.

"Ay, well. A young couple needs time to settle in, now don't they? You don't want the in-laws around every weekend. You'll understand that, James, when it's time."

It was an extraordinary thing to say, and I would have considered it simply a lie if he hadn't repeated it on other occasions. Everyone knew that he disapproved of the marriage and was bitterly disappointed that my father did not go to university. I remember seeing him when I was six, when my grandmother died — she would come to visit on her own, without him — and that, I think, was the only time until he showed up at our door. I was too young, really, to know, but those were bitter years. So his claim that he was staying away out of politeness was quite untrue — and yet he said it so easily, and was a man of such gravity, that it seemed to me that perhaps he believed it. My mother would not have let him get away with it, and so he avoided the subject entirely with her, which allowed them both to step around the pain and get on with it — an essential sort of behaviour in the adult world, it was becoming clear to me.

It was becoming clear too that something out of the ordinary was happening in my house. Grandfather took to shaving in the late afternoon as well as in the morning and putting on a new shirt and a black bow tie for when Mother arrived home, and more often than not a fresh vase of flowers would be on the table and Grandfather started quoting passages of poetry to her while they prepared the dinner. "Ae fond kiss, and then we sever; ae farewell and then forever," he would recite in his deep, stirring stage voice.

Grandfather was excitable in love, too jovial, off-balance, and I could imagine the glorious Colleen pulling him this way and that like a bouncy dog on a leash. But to see my mother do it — well, that was awful. It had been only months since Father's death and here she was laughing at this old man's jokes, preparing food with him, basking in his boyish gazes. I became a young Prince Hamlet, brooding and moping and glowering in shadows, and this unthinkable attraction between widow and father-in-law became yet another gaping hole in our household that we pretended wasn't there.

But I was approaching an age when a hole becomes far too fascinating to ignore; when the imperative is to creep to its edge and look down with a flashlight, to test the depths, to jump in and yell and wake everyone up! What were they thinking of? It was obvious he was reliving his time with Colleen, who had married someone else, who hadn't waited while he went to university, who had died in childbirth before he returned to the village to see her again. I saw the pictures in his album — there were fourteen of Colleen and three of my grandmother, and my mother looked a lot like Colleen. "What are you doing? What are you thinking of?" I felt like shouting. My father would have ordered him out of the house. No wonder they didn't speak to one another. I pounded the punching bag an hour every day and went for long, solitary walks and then hurried home in case they had gone over the edge. A terrible suspicion gripped me that I would come home one day and find them in bed, making the sounds that she and Father had made late at night. And so I took to entering the house as loudly as I could, shuffling and stamping my feet, calling hellos like a woodsman not wanting to run into a bear. Sure enough they would be together — but not in her bedroom, not in bed — in the kitchen, discussing a marinade, or she would be in his room with her eyes closed listening to his violin.

But I was not the only one with suspicions. My Great-aunt Harriet, Mother's father's sister, the last of her generation on that side of the family, came to visit six months after Father's death and was immediately suspicious. She was a powdered, imperious woman never able to quite sit still but vibrating constantly with age; when she spoke her lips quivered in time with the hanging folds of flesh on her neck. But her eyes were clear and she saw Grandfather's foolish expression when he looked at my mother. Within a week we were all invited to dinner at her home not too far out of town. She had also invited a widow, a friend of some six decades, and the widow's bachelor son, a chartered accountant whose remaining hair was cut respectably short, who wore thick glasses and whose face turned alarm-bell red for no reason.

"George has been with his firm for sixteen years," Harriet said — "Seventeen, actually," George added, blushing and sneaking a secret glance at my mother. "A very reputable firm," Harriet pushed on. "Father used to do business with them, didn't they, George?" "Some of our clients have been with us for generations," George said, and then Grandfather erupted with the *hhhrrrumpphhhh!* he sometimes used as a weapon. "Harriet — I am overcome with this dinner." Then, "You've been living at home all these years, is that right George?" and without waiting for an answer but shaking his head, "Well, it certainly speaks to great loyalty on your part."

As for Harriet's longtime friend, so carefully made up, her hands so nervous and afraid, Grandfather did not even look at her, speak to her, acknowledge that she was there. His comments were always directed to Harriet or to George ("Seventeen years with the *same* company — you must be the president by now, George!"), or to Mother in some whispered aside that she would laugh at.

The death-knell of the evening was sounded directly after dinner when Grandfather spotted a chessboard in the corner of the den. "George, man — do you play?" he asked, in a doubtful tone that implied a complete questioning of George's manhood. So the two retired, as did the ladies who gathered in the kitchen for a quick "swish" of the dishes and a long round of stories from Harriet and her friend's childhood. At one point the conversation turned to Grandfather and what exactly he was doing with his house on the coast. Mother mentioned that a disastrous business deal had left him "quite bereft — almost penniless, I would say," and Harriet's friend's enthusiasm visibly waned.

Grandfather kept George in the chess game for hours. He was an accomplished player but would not allow the younger man to make a bad move — "Heavens man, I don't think you want to do that!" Grandfather would say, putting George's knight back. "I'd have you going in two directions. Think about it some more. It's a contemplative game." And the pensive accountant, faced with an absorbing problem, would sink ever deeper into his stuffed chair.

Finally, at nine-thirty, Grandfather made three quick moves

to end the game and then stood up stretching and yawning. "Harriet, this has been a marvellous evening!" he announced. "But you know how it is with old men — I'm going to turn into a pumpkin very soon if I don't get my rest. It has been *so* nice to see you again, my dear."

How they laughed together on the way home, Grandfather and my mother. They were acting like children, which somehow seemed all right for Grandfather — old people are almost children again anyway — but Mother should have known better. She was beautiful and intelligent and funny and lonely, and Grandfather was so foggy-eyed and trusting when he looked at her. She should have had more restraint. She should have done something.

But when Great-aunt Harriet invited us for dinner again, this time with someone from the ladies' club and a gentleman who worked at the library, it was more of the same, although Harriet had managed to hide the chess set. "You've spent your whole life *reading*, man?" Grandfather asked, leaning across the table in disbelief. "Have you never done anything?" And while the poor man stammered, Harriet said, "Oh, Trafford, don't *blow* so hard," and the invited woman sat extraordinarily still in her peach dress, watching.

After dinner, since chess was not available, Grandfather waded into the other man's domain — books — but on his own terms. "I was left unsatisfied by Socrates's apology," he said. "I'm not sure that Plato reported it accurately. I'm not sure that he got the distinction between God and the Good quite measured. Do you find that?" and the poor librarian was on the spot. He was not a great conversationalist anyway, but Grandfather did not even let him get started. Instead he embarked on a series of classical quotations, of which his brain was full, driven in from reading the same few books over and over during his years at sea. More often than not the passages would have very little to do with the subject, but he delivered them magnificently, with fists clenched, his voice now a club, now a rapier, now a battle axe. When the librarian finally got to say that he preferred the "modern classics" like D.H. Lawrence to the Greeks, Grandfather rained all weapons upon him at once. "You prefer a worm-brained smut-monger to Plato and Aristotle?" he boomed. "Good Lord, man, why the sewer over the pinnacle? It's a wonder Lawrence could even sit down long enough to write, he did so much of his thinking through his penis! Ladies — I'm sorry. Perhaps we should change the topic."

And so Grandfather shifted into his other great love, Chaucer, and began to quote long passages in Middle English until it was time to go. He was especially fond of the racier sections of the Miller's and the Summoner's tales, but he had so cowed the librarian that his hypocrisy was not pointed out. He had bullied the man so badly that Harriet never had us to dinner again, which was perhaps Grandfather's goal in the first place. But Mother did not laugh with him on the way home, and the evening marked a subtle but important shift for the two of them.

It was not so long afterwards that Mother began coming home a little later than usual from work. Without explanation, two or three times a week she would not make it back in time to help Grandfather with the cooking. I can't remember how long this went on or the first time I noticed that her clothes smelled of cigarettes or when exactly her crying stopped at night. Time is a great mesmerizer, drawing us away from the point where we were fixed to somewhere different, somewhere unfixed, without our even knowing it. Moving so slowly, telling us what we want to hear, changing the coastline while our eyes are averted.

Neither Grandfather nor I wanted to know, and Mother

didn't want to tell us, so even though the clues were there we didn't put them together or else we found alternate solutions.

And then, with only the warning of these several months of unheeded clues, she suddenly brought home Lee. He was not a big man but he was muscular and free-moving and reminded me of my father in the thickness of his neck and the strength of his grip and the gentleness in his eyes. He and Grandfather stood for some minutes in the hallway, hands locked in a death-grip, the older man towering over the younger and yet not seeming any bigger. I've never seen any man return Grandfather's grip ounce for ounce the way that Lee did — in fact Grandfather was turning paler and paler, his grin fixed and strained. Neither man would look away first; finally Mother came back from the kitchen and said, "For heaven's sakes, honestly! Don't break one another's bones!"

Lee was wearing faded, well-loved jeans, a purple collarless cotton shirt, and running shoes that looked as battered and perfect as any pair of my own. I hated him immediately, as did Grandfather, who stood in his fine trousers and his new shirt with the high collar and his bow tie, donned as usual in anticipation of Mother's return.

"I wish you'd called me," he said to her, his voice a little thin. "I'd planned on sole for tonight but I didn't stock extra."

"Oh, that's all right," Mother replied, too easily, as if the world were not falling apart. "Lee and I brought some groceries. He's going to throw something together for us."

If she had hit Grandfather in the face with a plate she could not have been more cruel. But there it was — struck in his own domain, banished from the kitchen, while Mother and this new man chatted quietly and laughed and we losers sat glumly in the living room peeking in from time to time.

They had no shortage of things to say to each other but it was not getting-to-know-you sort of chat — it was the quiet, easy patter of people who have been day-to-day for some time now. Much worse was the way he leaned over her at the counter and put his hand on her hip *and she did not remove it*, and he said something to her, standing much closer than he needed to, *and she did not move away*.

Grandfather was sitting at the head of the table waiting to be served when chicken cordon bleu arrived with tiny perfect roast potatoes and baby carrots and a sauce that was like riding in a balloon on a sunny day with someone dazzling and lovely. I was prepared to hate the meal, but instead it was completely gone from my plate in minutes. By the time I came back with my extra helping I realized that Grandfather considered me a traitor and was going to plunge on in the battle alone.

"So," he said, clearing his throat and chewing his food slowly, as if making his way through shoe leather. "What do you call work, sir — if I might ask?"

"I'm a cabinet-maker," Lee said.

"Restorations? Antiques?"

"I only make new furniture," he said, not giving much away, wary. "And you, sir — you were a sailor for many years, is that right?" he asked.

"Marine engineer," Grandfather replied stiffly.

"You must have been in the war. Did you see service?"

Grandfather nodded. "A bit," he said, and then, stumbling in the effort to be modest, "five years, actually."

Lee's face beamed with admiration. "I bet you were in the North Atlantic."

"I ran a few convoys up there," Grandfather said, as humbly as he could. "Bloody cold. Our ship was so small it rolled in a heavy dew."

"Not a destroyer, then?"

"Good heavens, no. A little corvette."

"Did you ever hit a mine or — ?"

It did not take much prodding after all before the stories started to come out of the three times the *Phoenix Rising* seemed to be doomed to a watery grave, battered by the wind and waves, and how the crew rallied with the pumps and the blowtorches, and how Grandfather rigged up sea sails to reclaim the broken steering. He sat tall and full and confident again at the table, was even able to compliment the younger man's cooking. "Of course I'm not much of a judge. In the war the rations were designed to line your stomach with lead so that anything at all would be suitable. Salt cod and prunes for months on end."

Renewed, Grandfather practically commanded Lee to share a game of chess with him. "Just a short one. James, you help your mother with the dishes." The men retired to the living room and Grandfather produced his tiny travelling chess set that had pitched and rolled with him all those years in the war and some years afterwards in the merchant marine. Mother shook her head to see them huddled over their game but was too happy to get upset. She seemed to float through the kitchen, humming to herself.

There was no talk from the other room. Grandfather was not correcting Lee's moves in order to prolong the game — he was focused on the jugular from the beginning, playing swiftly, decisively, betraying a confident anger in the way he moved his pieces to their spots on the board, grimly capturing a pawn, a knight, a rook. He wasn't taking time to think — the moves were already calculated. He did not look at the younger man.

So by the time the dishes were done Grandfather had sliced away a good portion of his opponent's army. Lee had captured a few men as well, but I gathered they were only taken in losing exchanges. The game couldn't possibly last much longer although I had the impression that Grandfather wanted to do as much damage as possible before finishing him off. Not just defeat but annihilation was the aim.

And then a bishop, a lonely, forgotten bishop of Lee's somehow crossed the length of the board, threading between pawns and other obstacles to strike at Grandfather's queen, which had been busy wiping out an important corner of the younger man's defences. It happened wordlessly, in harmony with the rest of the game, but like an assassin's knife it changed everything in an instant. Grandfather let out a quick breath of air, set his jaw, and did not say a word. But his eyes worried about the board, flashing from move to move.

He wasn't going to annihilate his opponent. He might not even win. The battle was going to be much longer than expected. And so he fought on with his rump army, deprived of his greatest weapon but determined more than ever to claw his way back. He was not one to resign; his eyes blazed in the way they must have when his corvette was sinking, when the tarpaulins were being ripped from the lifeboats and German submarines lurked off the bow and the deck listed in the cold Atlantic night. *Man the pumps! Patch the hull! Fire those guns! Depth charges, first aid, keep the engines running!*

Grandfather shoved Lee's men all over the board and yet he could not quite finish them off, and Lee's queen would sail onto the scene like a battleship confronting a bunch of canoes. Grandfather kept himself alive, but not much more; the best he could hope for was a draw.

Which he would not propose himself and which he did not even get. Mother came into the room wearing a brand-new silky dress, her face freshly made up, her coat in her hands. We all turned and gaped, she was so beautiful. "I think we're going to be late," she said, and Lee was up in an instant. Grandfather did not rise.

"It's been a real pleasure meeting you," Lee said as he put on his jacket.

"Good night," Mother said, pulling open the door.

And then they were gone.

Grandfather did not move for a long time. He kept staring at the door. Finally he rose and very deliberately put away the pieces of his chess set — carved marine ivory, yellowing with age. Then he went downstairs and pulled on the boxing gloves and slammed the big bag for over an hour, his massive blows shaking the house, his breathing slow and deep and murderous. Then he went out for a walk. When he got back he was disappointed that Mother had not yet returned. He kept looking at his watch — ten-thirty? A quarter to eleven? Five minutes past? I stayed with him in his room as he played the violin, slowly and with sadness, until after midnight. Still she wasn't back. Finally he put it away and slumped on the bed and said, "You should go. School tomorrow. Don't tell your mother I kept you up."

I turned to leave, but at the door he said, "I remember nights at sea. During the war especially. It was so boring and so lonely. Sometimes it was frightening, but at least you did things then. When there was nothing happening . . ." The thought seemed to trail off. I took another step. He said, "She would come to visit me sometimes at night. She would sit on my bunk, just on the edge — ay, nothing happened, mind you, it was all above board. We just talked. She would tell me all about her aunt — now what was her name? — who was always coming up with presentable young men for her."

"Who, Grandfather?" I asked.

"Colleen," he said, shaken, as if he didn't expect to see me there, although he had been talking to me all along.

Mother came home the next morning when we were sitting at breakfast, Grandfather in the middle of his usual basin of plain porridge and glass of hot water. Her dress was a little rumpled and her face a little dazed, and she smiled like the sun, newly risen.

"Good morning," she said, kissing us, and then she went upstairs to change for work.

THREE

Grandfather was not a man to admit impediments; he ignored them, denied their existence and carried on regardless. He was entirely civil to Lee, and even friendly on two or three occasions, although the effort was obviously wearing. What Grandfather didn't admit was that Lee was a rival, that there was a situation here. Instead he tucked in his chin as if he were striding ahead through a snowstorm, the elements be damned.

Mother was spending two or three nights a week with Lee, who had a small apartment above his workshop. She would not say to us, "By the way, I won't be in tonight." Grandfather would pace and mope and stare through the window into the blackness until after midnight but would always leave on the kitchen light as if Mother would probably be wanting a late snack. Most of the time we would be at breakfast when she returned, shining and rumpled. Grandfather would say something like, "I thought we'd have a little fish for tonight — is that all right?" and Mother would pause as if the question had been on her mind for some time. "Fine, yes, that would be great. Is today your math test?" she would ask me, on her way up the stairs to get ready for the office.

Grandfather's face, set in stone, would return to his oatmeal. When Mother came back down the stairs it would be as if she had just arisen, had slept the night with us, under our roof, had not spent it, little of it sleeping, with a stranger.

"Ay, your mother's a fine version of a woman," he would say to me after school as we went through our training on the punching bags. And immediately after saying it he would slam the big bag, shuddering the rafters of the house. "What do you think of Lee?" I would ask sometimes, and Grandfather would continue as if he hadn't heard the question. *Wham! Wham! Wham!* "Ay, James, it's not the length of the punch," he would say. "It's all in your legs anyway. Look at Jack Dempsey. I've never seen another man punch from the legs the way he did."

And then for dinner, which he slaved over, preparing the sauce, gently frying the fish, polishing the silver so that it gleamed in candlelight, he would be wearing his fine white shirt and bow tie, his face newly shaven for my mother's arrival.

"Oh, Trafford, you've outdone yourself!" she would say, her face gleaming as if she herself were polished, as if she wouldn't go and betray us all in just a few hours, as if the family wasn't a joke, a crumbling façade, a leaky boat on temporarily calm waters.

"I was running around most of the day looking for a

property survey," she might say, biting into the fish and making her face look dreamy. "It was done about twenty years
ago and there have been nine owners since. Could I find a
copy of the survey? God, every lawyer that I contacted —
and they are such bastards sometimes . . ." and I would stop
chewing, because Mother — my *real* mother — would never
swear, and certainly not at the dinner table. This was obviously Lee's influence. But Grandfather would be clinging to
every word, laughing at the slightest joke, basking in the
beauty of the candlelight on her face.

I was not under the same influence. "Why don't you
come home at night?" I asked her bluntly, in a rare moment
when Grandfather left us alone. "What if a burglar came?
What if you got hit by a car? This is your house — you're
supposed to sleep here!"

"I know this is difficult for you," she said, and I cut her
off, using my new thirteen-year-old body to look her straight
in the eye. "I didn't say it was difficult. I just want to know.
Why can't it be like it was?"

"Because things change," she said in an inadequate voice.

"Are you going to marry him?"

She didn't answer.

"Is he supposed to be my new father? Is that it? Well, he
isn't. My father's dead!"

The situation was compounded by my own difficulties in
love. My heart had been shanghaied by Mirele, whose father
was a diplomat working for the time being in industry. She
had come to our school via Sydney, Hong Kong and Lon-
don, with black, unruly hair cut jarringly short in a time
when *all* girls had long hair parted in the middle and
brushed straight down to their backsides. She had a white,
sculpted, troubled face, and hazel eyes with little flecks in
them that looked metallic, and long, slender limbs, and her

impertinent nipples poking out at her shirt in cool weather compensated entirely for her boyish near-lack of breasts. We walked along the same route to school, and she was the one who started talking to me. She said, "Is this the way to Wigwam School?" and I said, "Waghorn," and she said, "Whatever," in that way of hers that could reduce nations' capitals to the status of remote villages with the turn of a phrase.

Mirele was two years older than me — light years it seemed, at that age, when I was so bottled up inside that having a conversation with a bona fide member of the opposite sex happened about as rarely as an earthquake and was just as terrifying. We lived in a claustrophobic suburb of a rather conservative town, or perhaps it was just being thirteen that was so closed and conservative. Almost everybody in my class had been in my class the year before, and before that, and before that, starting when the boys were tiny tyrants running around the playground with frogs in our hands looking for dresses in which to deposit them, and the girls were circled like covered wagons, skipping and talking, endlessly talking. And then cauldrons were stirred deep inside us that caused mysterious patches of hair to sprout in unlikely places, that lowered voices and grew breasts and produced body odour, and that nobody could talk about. Girls were the Other, a closed society of whispering, giggling, note-writing beings forever noticing and not letting on what they knew. Actually talking to one of them meant physically approaching a whole cluster, singling one out, and figuring out what to say before embarrassment struck you down like dengue fever.

(*Struck you down like dengue fever* was something that Mirele was always saying, as in, "Oh, that toad-brain Lawson — I wanted to strike him down like dengue fever!" I had no idea what it was, but it sounded awful.)

Mirele was outside that world. It was not difficult at all to start a conversation with her. We took the same route; if we were not quite synchronized she would wait, or I would wait, or she would catch up to me. And I would hardly have to open my mouth, because Mirele had far more than enough to say for both of us, and it was in my nature to listen.

"I have period two today with Lawson, that *lech*. He came up behind me — it was Wednesday — and *put his hand on my shoulder*. GOD! — it was like being touched by a pod-person — I hate it when people make you feel completely flammy — do you know what I mean?" I would nod. "No, you don't know what I mean. Anyway, my Mom has found a new therapist, *finally*, but I caught her yesterday with those pills I was telling you about —"

And on and on until our twenty minutes was up. Her father was having an affair with some new woman Mirele had not been able to track yet; her mother was barely inflated and floating about two feet under the surface, an apparent wreck of a woman completely enslaved by alcohol, sedatives, boredom and menopause, who told her daughter everything and then swore her to silence, who was forever taking correspondence courses on the human condition and dropping them before she could finish and then signing up for another. Mirele had a universe of things to talk about, and I drank it in. And then when I got to my school, Waghorn Elementary, I would turn left and Mirele would continue on to Waghorn High, a bare fifty yards further that might as well have been the Atlantic Ocean.

I had it figured out in my head. She could not possibly love me now because she was so old and I was so young. I would have to wait, hang on grimly, patiently. I would build up my body, train my mind, become worthy of her. And sometime she would not be so old, and I would not be so young, and everything would be different, and we would have started by being friends.

And so I rose with Grandfather at six, working out in the living room in my pyjamas with the iron coil dumbbells that his grandfather had given to him and grunting through sit-ups and stretches and isometric exercises designed by Charles Atlas to keep bullies from kicking sand in the faces of former wimps. After school we stripped to the waist and punished the punching bags downstairs, rocking the big bag with crippling blows, dancing around the little one, bobbing and weaving, rattling the house with our masculinity. But after three months of this strict regimen I seemed only skinnier, wearier and more ragged, and my joints hurt at night, and I ached in the mornings when I walked to school.

Mirele did not do all the talking, of course. Sometime in those first few months she became extremely interested in the bizarre situation at my home, which seemed as warped and unhealthy and therefore as fascinating as her own. Toxic families became part of what we had in common, and I felt a sense of relief when I talked about how civil they all were to one another, Lee with his firm handshake and reverential eyes and how he kissed my mother in the kitchen when he thought no one was watching, and Grandfather, cold and polite as a statue but I had seen him rip the big bag from its moorings. Surely it would not be long before he thrashed the younger man in the way that he deserved for pretending to be so deferential.

For loving my mother.

For not being my father.

Mirele was especially interested in Grandfather, and so I told her all about Colleen, the Scottish lass he had loved so futilely all his life and still talked about as if she were a poem etched in his soul. When Mirele seemed to think that was a tale of extraordinary romance I told her about my grand-mother, a tiny, fiery woman who raised three sons and slogged through four decades of loveless marriage, with Grandfather away so much at sea and so cold and aloof and bitter when he was at home. She would come to visit us sometimes, alone because of the feud between Father and Grandfather, and she would talk for ages about Trafford's impossible habits and disruptive ways — his snoring and his silences and his sanctimony over exercise and diet. They had managed to live separate lives for such a long time that when he retired from the merchant marine and was suddenly home to stay they could not get along but fought over every-thing, Grandmother attacking like a fierce little bird while Grandfather stayed monolithically, maddeningly calm.

"I don't know why people get married," I remember Mirele saying to me. "They turn into such fossils. I will never get married personally. I'll probably just have lots of affairs."

It would have been quite all right with me if I had been her first. She was so worldly and feminine and mysterious with her long tight pants and her black walking boots and her Indian cloth purse that hung from her shoulder. In the months at her school she had not made a single friend but stood out utterly in dress and attitude. Why not someone younger? Was I not trainable? Had I not grown a verifiable half-inch taller than she was in the time we had known each other?

But I had no idea how to begin. While she was talking about the house servant in Hong Kong who had to be sent away because her mother found out what her father had been doing, I kept wondering how one does it. How do you begin? How do you know? Why could I tell her everything about that night soon after my father's death when Mother lost her wedding ring and nearly tore the hair from her head in grief and despair, and yet not be able to ask her "out," whatever "out" was? Was it going to the coffee shop to have something other than coffee because I wasn't old enough yet to drink it?

(She probably drank coffee. She was old enough.)

Was it going to a movie?

(I would have to ask my mother for the money. And to drive us. And to pick us up again.)

Was it going for a walk?

(Grandfather always went for walks with Colleen in the hills above Aberdeen, on the North Sea coast, through gales and piercing rain. She never got tired. She never stopped talking. She never lost the full bloom of beauty because she died so young, the bride of another man. Going for walks was a tricky business.)

I kept trying to think of exactly what to say, and how to say it, and how to react when she said no, so that we both would know that it didn't matter, that I was in for the long haul, that I was training my body and my mind and someday would not be so much younger. It was so hard that I never quite got the words out; they ran over and over in my head in a looping speech that didn't turn off at night but continued regardless, eating up more and more of my circuits.

I should just wait another year until I'm at least in the same school, I decided. By then I'll have the wording down. I'll know what to say. I'll be older.

(Is this what happened to Grandfather? Did he just keep walking and walking and never get to the point where you stop and hold hands and look out at the sunset and kiss like you are supposed to when you are young and in love and the world is just beginning? What if you never said the right thing at the right time? Would it just not happen?)

And then, when I had definitely decided that I should not

say anything until at least two years or when my biceps exceeded eighteen inches (whichever came first), she asked me. It was February and the ground was frozen and the sky was nearly dark even though it was still afternoon. I had started to walk down my street, muffled in a parka, and she turned to me, wearing her stylish coat that looked about as warm as tissue paper, and said, "Look, it's my birthday Saturday and my parents are making me have a party. Are you going to come?" It sounded like having a birthday party was only slightly more attractive than suicide, but she tempered her tone a bit and added, "You can meet my flammy relatives."

And so I arrived at her door on Saturday night. I had a present, a new album by Trunkless CloudMoon, an Australian band that combined elements of traditional Celtic music with acid rock to produce a singular sound that Mirele would rave about as the only music worth listening to. And I was wearing a plaid jacket that had become too small but nevertheless poked out under the waist of my ski jacket, and a purple turtleneck that was rumpled and scratchy, but I had got it from the bottom of my drawer, so it was probably clean, and a pair of corduroys that were clean, pressed and relatively fashionable but which had a zipper that was forever sliding down.

There at the door was Mrs. Lewis, tall and stately, with beautiful blonde hair perfectly set and shining and a blue dress that gleamed in the warm light of the foyer and kind, understanding eyes. "You must be James," she said, beckoning me in. "Can I take your coat? I hope you haven't had to come far — it's so cold out. You go to Esmirelda's school, is that right?" Mrs. Lewis asked.

"Who?" I said.

"*Mother*," Mirele said, the word cutting like a stroke from a Samurai sword, and Mrs. Lewis looked between us in that dumbfounded way that parents have.

"At any rate, won't you come in?" Mrs. Lewis asked me, and I followed her into the first of what I thought to be three living rooms, beautifully furnished and lined with books, oil paintings on every wall.

("My parents are so status-oriented," Mirele had said to me countless times.)

There were no other guests. Mr. Lewis was waiting in the third living room, a Cary Grant of a man with jet-black hair, his blue blazer and grey pants and black polished shoes looking as though they had been bought that afternoon. "Very pleased to meet you, James," he said. His hand was big and warm and firm, but not crushing in the way that Grandfather's was, and his skin was tanned and glowing and smelled slightly of some rich oil.

The four of us sat in tall-backed chairs around a fire holding our drinks, a ginger ale for me, a small glass of wine for Mirele, something stronger for her parents. Mirele's older brother, Reginald, was out of town that weekend at a fencing tournament, and I gathered that Mr. Lewis had been something of a champion himself as a youth. It was startling to see him, and Mrs. Lewis too, expecting as I was from all Mirele had told me warty, pock-marked, crippled personalities whose neuroses and failures would somehow be as obvious as cracks in the walls. But no — they were elegant and kind and funny and graceful, and it was very adult, somehow, to dine with them on roast lamb beneath a real chandelier and sip ginger ale from a wine glass and look across at Mirele, who had her mother's eyes and her father's cheekbones, and who barely touched her food, and who said so little she almost seemed shy.

"I'm sorry to drag you through all that," she said to me afterwards when we went downstairs into the den. It had dark padded furniture and pillows arranged around a television set we wouldn't have been able to get through the door, much less afford. Mirele insisted the stereo system was "junky," but it sounded to me like it could bring down the whole neighbourhood if the volume knob was turned to more than a fraction of its potential.

"My parents are really hung up on traditional stuff. They're just — they're just hung up on tradition in general. It would have been a lot worse if you hadn't come."

"Worse?"

"They're worried about my social development," she said, making her voice sound uppity.

"I think they're really nice," I said.

"Well, they are if you don't have to live with them. I mean, it's all this façade. They're really, like, pod-people inside. They're diplomats, they're all fucked up, but they look great. That's their job."

And so we listened to Trunkless CloudMoon, both sides, three times, and I watched the soft light on her cheek and the pointy marks on her black shirt over her nipples, and I wondered how you go about kissing a girl, whether you have to make a speech first or clear your throat or brush your teeth. It was hard going; there didn't seem to be a trail, it was dark, and I couldn't see which way to go.

In the end I ran out of time. Mrs. Lewis called down the stairs just as Mirele was wondering what else to put on the stereo, and Mirele went up to answer the phone. I waited for quite a while and then crept up the stairs to see what had happened. Mr. Lewis had already gone to bed. Mrs. Lewis was drinking a glass of milk in her robe in the kitchen and said, "Oh dear — I thought you'd left already. Jeremy has called from England. She's going to be hours. I'll just get her. Esmirelda!" she said, going off to look for her. But I didn't wait. My jacket and boots were on in a moment and the night air was so cold I felt like I had fallen overboard in the North Atlantic and these were my two minutes before death.

Grandfather was still up, waiting for Mother. He heard the sounds in the hall and said, "I was wondering if you'd —" and when he saw it wasn't Mother he stopped, his face having trouble adjusting to the disappointment. "Ay, boy — is that you? I thought you were in bed. What have you been up to now?"

"Nothing," I said.

"Out chasing a girl?" I walked past him and up the stairs, and I lay in bed, heavy as a corpse beneath a mile of ocean. She has struck me down like dengue fever, I thought, as I looked at the light under the crack in the door, which was Grandfather staying up for someone he wouldn't admit that he loved — not in that way — yet would never give up, and would never have.

No, Grandfather was not a man to admit impediments, and neither was I, and that was the beginning of my sorrows.

FOUR

About a year after my father's death my jaw welded shut and would not open for anything. It was evident one morning after what must have been a long night of bad dreams. I was a teeth-grinder anyway and was used to a little soreness in the morning, but this was the complete solidification of a pre-viously working joint.

Grandfather was already up, pretending to read the pa-per while he had his porridge. It was one of the mornings that Mother was away at Lee's, and he was doing his best to be calm and nonjudgemental when she walked through the door. He never quite got this terrible effort right, but it so preoccupied him that he didn't really notice I was there.

Mother was late that morning and didn't have time to say much, so I left for school without anyone's having noticed that I hadn't said a word. Along the way I did not talk to Mirele — our friendship had never recovered after her birthday party. Maybe a good talk would have cleared things up, but we didn't have it and so they got muddier and mud-dier. For probably a week afterwards we missed each other on our walks to and from school, long enough for me to con-template the fact that, she now being sixteen and I still only thirteen, I was losing ground. I would see her and put my head down and speed up, because it was up to her to apolo-gize. But she never caught up, and now after so many weeks the act of ignoring her enlarged her presence until she trailed like a dirigible. I turned off at my elementary school, she continued on to her high school, and then I went through an entire day without saying a word. It was enor-mously easy because my class had thirty-five students, I was quiet by nature anyway, and almost everyone who liked me did so because I listened and knew when to nod.

If I never spoke again in my whole life, no one would no-tice.

At home I listened to Grandfather and Mother prattling as they made the dinner together, and I went to my room. It seemed to me that I was in a prison, that I was forever wait-ing to get older — that when you are older you can reach to other people for solace and love, but not when you are thirteen and have no experience to count on. Not only was the future murky and far away, but the past was somehow evaporating. My father had been dead only a year and yet it was very hard to picture him now. He had had a beard, big hands, quick, lively eyes. But what colour were they? What shape was his head? Did he hold his shoulders square and erect like Grandfather? How big were his feet (mine had become the size of flippers)? And what did his laugh sound like? I couldn't remember if he had an Adam's apple — it seemed to me he must have, because Grandfather's was so large and active. Though they were different in many ways, the older man was replacing the younger in my mind. We had family albums but it was Father who always took the pictures, and now only a few shots of him remained — mostly wedding photos, with his hair short and no beard and his borrowed jacket too big. It didn't look like him. Was Mother really the taller of the two? Then I would be taller than him now, but I couldn't imagine that, because he was always such a large man and I was always so small.

That night we had meatloaf, which I could not get into my mouth. The next day at the doctor's it became apparent that the problem "was not serious," that it would probably go away in a few days — was everything all right at home? — and that nothing could be done. I was at a stressful age, the doctor said. Most of his cases were actually young girls, he said, usually at exam time. There was nothing to worry about.

"Yes, thank you, doctor," Mother said.

Clamped tight and painful in the mornings, after a few days my jaw would at least loosen up so that by dinnertime I could manage, if only slowly, to chew some meat. Soup, Jell-O, scrambled eggs, ice cream — there was plenty of soft food to eat, and I adapted to my handicap. I especially liked the attention from my mother — she stayed a whole week without once going to Lee's. I liked not having to talk. I liked wandering from room to room like a ghost with responsibility lifted but curiosity intact.

But I wanted my father back.

I wanted something to hang onto. Mother had sent all his clothes to the Salvation Army — he had had a battered leather hockey jacket that was exactly the sort of thing I needed to have, and now that it was gone I mourned its loss as well. But I was being silent, my life would pass in noble anonymity, and so I could not say to Mother, "Is there anything that he left — a pocket knife, a razor, a watch? Did he write any letters? Was there a journal that I could read?"

Instead I looked for these things secretly, creeping about the house when no one else was there, going through his closet, through Mother's dresser, through the boxes in the basement. But Mother was nothing if not thorough in her sweep of Father's things, and Father was a man who shed encumbrances, whose desk was clear at the end of the day. There was his workshop, of course, with the tools all hanging in their places on the board, but even those Grandfather had got to and scrubbed shiny. Now not even Father's grease remained.

I did find a book, a journal of sorts, in one of Mother's drawers. It was full of Father's tiny, packed handwriting, and my heart leapt when I opened it, for it might have been exactly what I was looking for — an opening into his life. Yet passage after passage read, "8 gross, light grey ordered for Fairweather Street. Holes in front section — $350. Talk to Mrs. G. about vents." They were his roofing notes, not his thoughts about loving my mother, about the arrival of his son, about what it felt like to walk at night and watch the moon and make love and look across at us at breakfast with winter frost safely outside and the kettle boiling here in the kitchen and the radio playing some song that reminded him of something else.

I didn't know my father at all, and as I wandered through my days of silence it became evident I didn't know anybody. Grandfather sat alone at night reading or playing his violin, but softly now, so as not to disturb anyone else. (Why didn't he teach his son the violin, so that his son could have taught me, so that I would have known how to play it by now?) He was thinking about his Colleen, I knew — but what, exactly, beyond the sketchy few stories he had told us, was he thinking about her? Was he reaching for her breast, and if he was, what kind of breast was it, and what did her lips feel like, or did he ever even kiss her, and if he didn't, why not? And Mother, preoccupied with her work and with this new man she was afraid to bring home, with getting on with things after Father's sudden collapse — what was it like really inside her life? When she made love with Lee did she think of Father? How did she feel the night she met Father, when she looked across the room through the darkness and the smoke and the whirling bodies and saw the young man sitting at the table not talking to his buddies, not drinking his beer, but just looking at her?

They danced, and Father asked her to marry him. It was absurd, but six months later they were married. That was the family story which I never questioned, how exactly they got from the A of dancing together to the Z of being married without seeming to go through all those other letters. What did Mother think of this boy-man six years younger, barely twenty, stammering in front of her? What was it that happened to him in that darkened room when he saw her? What was it that happened to both of them, that made them change course so extremely and carry on despite all good sense and be so happy for their time together? Was there a furnace burning between them, and did she feel it immediately, when they danced, or did Father have to try again and again and again?

What did Mother think of all this now?

I didn't know. The very engines that had produced me had passed just as swiftly and were now unknowable. My father had vanished without a trace. The one place where I seemed to find a little bit of him, to feel a tiny wind of the man he used to be, was on the rooftop. It was where he was the most comfortable, where he could be tall and survey life among the quiet chimneys, the broken shingles, the weathered skin of protection between families and the sky.

I know people who have seen ghosts of their dead relatives, who turned the corner into the living room and there they were. I'm sure it happens, and if Father's ghost had been anywhere it would have been on a rooftop.

So I would sit on the roof and commune with Father, and sometimes I could feel something of him there, and sometimes it was just plain cold. I wouldn't have gone so often if I hadn't noticed that, with my back to the chimney and my head craned just so, I could see between the tops of two large maples and across several houses and backyards directly into Mirele's window. It was too far to see clearly, but it thrilled me somehow to feel that connection, to see the light turn on and feel a beam between us. After peering for quite a long time I could just make out that the curtains were open and she was sitting at her desk directly behind the window.

And that was all I could see until the next evening, when her face became much clearer with the help of Grandfather's field glasses. They were a tiny German pair, a souvenir from the war, cased in battered brass with lenses so clear and powerful they seemed to transport me just outside her window — I could see her white hand reaching up to smooth back her wild black hair, and the intentness of her eyes as she read the page, and the way her lip curled in when she was thinking.

And so life corrupts our motives. What had begun as a quest to know my father turned into a spying mission on the girl I loved so painfully from a distance. I wanted now to talk to her on the way to school, but she was changing like the seasons, winning friends now, filling out, growing older much faster than I seemed to be. Boys were hanging around her, and she was not scaring them off. Once I passed her on the way home as she was walking with one of them — a mastodon of a senior with squidgy eyes — and she looked directly at me, but there was not even a flicker of recognition, not even, "Yes — you were the little boy I used to walk to school with. How quaint to see you." At night she would sit at her desk and suddenly raise her eyes and look directly out the window, entirely lost in secret thoughts.

I missed her stories most of all, the way she would start talking even before I had caught up to her. "I think my mother knows," she would say. "I walked into the room and she was looking out the window with her back to him, clutching her drink like it was a life preserver, you know, sort of like this, with this grubile expression, and he was holding his drink like this and looking at a totally different angle — I mean, it was so symbolic of their whole marriage, and I just walked in like, *excuse me, I'm just the child, are we eating dinner tonight?*" There was nothing she wouldn't talk about, and it was intoxicatingly adult to listen to it all and nod understandingly.

When she was walking now with her friends, with the

mastodon, she hardly said anything, just looked about like a princess.

Father died on May the fourth. On the anniversary my jaw was still sore — it had been nearly three weeks since I could move it freely. On the actual day we went out in the rain and stood by the river where, against the law, we had dumped his ashes the year before, tipped the urn over while standing on a large rock near a fast-flowing part. I'd imagined that the ashes would be light and float away, but the fine, heavy powder sank immediately and sat in a lump on the bottom. I hadn't gone back to the spot in a whole year, partly out of fear that the lump would still be there, pretending to be my father.

It wasn't. Mother and Grandfather and I stood together looking down. Lee didn't come. I don't know whether he was too busy or Mother hadn't asked him. I was happy he wasn't there. It wouldn't have felt right. Grandfather opened up his immense black umbrella that he had bought in New York City in 1953, and it was big enough to cover us.

I expected Grandfather to say something because he had missed the funeral, but it was Mother who did most of the talking. She said, "I don't know if I ever told you, James. But this is the spot where I finally agreed to marry your father. It was the middle of winter. So cold you could hardly walk. One of my girlfriends woke me up and said, 'It's Romeo again. Don't you guys ever take a break?'"

Mother's hands were shoved into her pockets and her eyes were fixed on the water.

"I said, 'What are you doing here? It's two o'clock in the morning!' And he said, 'Come on, get your coat on, I want to show you something.' It was just — it was the coldest night of the year. Cars were freezing. There was supposed to be a blizzard on the way. And so I put on my coat and he took me to this spot. It was covered in snow and very dangerous. The wind was . . . like nails, but I didn't feel a thing. Being near him was like being in a warm air pocket. We walked right up to the edge, and then onto this rock. It was so cold the whole river was frozen over except for this one section that was bubbling on right through the ice. One slip, I could have fallen in — I remember it looked black and cold. But I had this feeling it didn't matter what happened — he'd always catch me. He loved me so much."

She was crying now as she looked down. "Your father, James . . . he pointed to this stretch of water that was still going, that wasn't frozen . . . and he said, 'That's us. That's you and me. That's what we are.'"

We got back in the car. On the way home the rain picked up and soon was driving so hard the wipers couldn't keep the windshield clear. Grandfather pulled off the road to wait it out. We didn't say anything. Mother fingered her wedding ring, and Grandfather looked out the window. Finally the rain let up enough and he started the engine and we went on.

At home there was a letter waiting for me, unstamped and a little wet. I didn't receive many letters. There was only one person it could have been from. She wrote, "I remember you telling me this was the day. How are you feeling? I think I read somewhere, 'There is no death really, there's just morning, then the night.' I don't know who the quote is from. Actually, I don't know anything about the subject at all. P.S. — It feels like ages since you talked to me."

She didn't sign her name — just a small M in the bottom corner. And she didn't write, "With love," or, "I'm sorry." But she had walked through the rain to bring it to me, and the moment I read it a great weight fell away. For the first time in weeks my jaw felt unbound, perfect, restored by a piece of paper. Not a roof of course, it seems to me now as I remember it, but perhaps a rafter, suspended in the air by whatever that was — the yearning reach of love, the blessing and the curse of it, my father's gift to me.

FIVE

"I found out who it is," she said, suddenly there the morning after her note, ending our months of silence. "*Finally*, this unbelievable *snake woman* from the company who wears — you won't believe this — lizardskin pants that are so tight they make her eyeballs bulge. At least I think it was the pants that were doing it. I saw them in the hallway upstairs . . . *touching* . . . and Dad had this sort of *politician's* expression — *the money has entirely been accounted for and there is no need for a special inquiry at this time* . . . how's your Mom anyway, is she still sleeping with that guy?"

Yes, she was, and she still rarely brought him home, and Grandfather was still jealous, and it felt like losing a load of cement to talk about it. And while we were talking that funny thing happened to time, the way that it did with Mirele. Almost before it began it seemed the walk was already over — I turned into my school and she went on to hers. No arrangements were made, but she was waiting for me on the walk home. She wasn't surrounded by doting seniors, and though there was nothing about our families we wouldn't talk about, not a word was mentioned about her birthday party months before. I never asked her who Jeremy was, and she never told me. It was all stuffed into the closet and forgotten. If Mirele wouldn't open it neither would I. It was enough to be with her.

Now with spring coming and the snow disappearing and graduation barely months away, I could walk with Mirele and concentrate on the coming world of high school. With each day we shed layers of clothes, and Mirele emerged more womanly than she had been in the fall. The lines were turning into curves; her shoulderblades were rounding out; her nipples, still wonderfully evident through thin fabric in a cool breeze, were beginning to be mounted now on real breasts contained within a bra (the contours of which I memorized, as if trying to read a letter through the envelope by holding it to the light.) And her face was lovely, cheeks fresh and rounded and eyes dark and cool and her black hair framing it differently every time the wind blew. From the distance of a few feet her skin looked impossibly soft, and she smelled womanly. In a time of short skirts and long hair, she wore short hair and skirts of Indian cotton so long they trailed the ground, exposing occasional glimpses of pointy leather boots that laced, it seemed, all the way up her calves.

"I just know they're hoping they won't have to tell me," she would say. "It's like we're all pod-people or something. We walk around on automatic — 'Yes, please, can I have some more tapioca?' — and everybody sitting together and nobody says, 'Dad, are you screwing the snake woman?' God — they'd die of a heart attack. Their faces would turn to rock and fall off. Instead it's pass the soma — *some of us are adults and some of us aren't, and until we're all adults and a number of us have moved away, we're all continuing with this charade.* I think the day I step out of that house she's going to take an axe and hack him to pieces and I'm going to have to read about it on the subway somewhere."

Pressed to the glass of the adult world, we were both hungrily looking in, and if no invitations were forthcoming, at least we could watch together. Then a terrible thing happened, a cruel and arbitrary event. Graduation came, school ended, and our daily excuse to get together disappeared. It hadn't occurred to me, but without school there would be no walk, and without a walk there was no Mirele. What to do? My heart raced with the question day and night.

Everything was changing, including my body. Hair was growing . . . down there. My voice was low one word, high the next. I couldn't get used to where things were anymore — lampstands were suddenly in the way; my feet found the legs of tables as I walked past; clothes that were fine three months ago now were ridiculously short. I could see over the refrigerator; I could bump my head on the landing; Grandfather was not so impossibly tall anymore. Objects fell from my hands arbitrarily — plates on their way to the dinner table collided with the stove; cups of tea sloshed as if I were on the deck of a rolling ship; garbage en route to the curb somehow struck the corner of the car and spilled all over the driveway. Even the telephone was my enemy.

"Just call her," a voice would say, whenever I was near the phone, and my body would race with adrenaline. "No one is in the kitchen. Now's the time. Just do it." So I would open up the telephone book to check her number, which I had memorized anyway, but what if I got it wrong? Before dialling I would write down on the little pad beside the phone, *Mirele — Hi*, because what if I couldn't get started? Then I would have to look up the phone number again, and pick up the receiver and put it down while Grandfather walked through the kitchen pretending to be preoccupied. Before I dialled I would decide to just run through a bit of a rehearsal. "Hi — Mirele!" I would say in my head. "I was just wondering —"

What was I wondering?

Grandfather would walk into the kitchen and stand in front of the calendar, motionless.

I would put down the phone and leave, and then come back to rescue the piece of paper that said *Mirele — Hi* on it, in case someone found it and knew.

Knew what?

That I was succumbing to the disease. That whatever it was that drove Mother out until morning and kept Grandfather awake in bed had got me too. That it was so strong I couldn't even pick up the telephone.

So I took up running. After dinner, when the house was quiet, and Grandfather was playing the violin, I would lace on my running shoes and slip out shirtless into the warm summer air. My route drifted through several parks and neighbourhoods, wound its way past the church and fire station and the two schools, along the river and under the bridge and through the woods and out into the meadow where the footing was always wet. Finally I would run down the lane that led past Mirele's house. However tired I was by then my stride would pick up; my back would straighten and my shoulders relax and I would let the roar of the crowd in the final lap of the Olympic marathon pull me around the bend, past the fourth place man, into the medals, picking up the silver, stretching it out, the gold in sight, only a few more seconds to break the world record . . .

I couldn't really look around to see if anyone was home, if she happened to be out on the porch, if her light was on upstairs. It was all a blur in the corner of my eye, the wash of the crowd in the stadium. But it seemed reasonable to me that, if I went by every night, at some point or other she would see me and know what an athlete I was becoming. And that would be enough.

So I continued for some weeks, but, though my store of Olympic medals increased nightly, I seemed to be no further ahead.

I went back to the telephone. I didn't bother looking up the number. I didn't write out my opening two words. I dialled in the darkness, leaning against the telephone table. It took several seconds — almost forever — to connect, and then just as it started ringing, Grandfather walked in and turned on the light and started looking at the calendar.

"Ay, lad, are you calling somebody?" Grandfather asked, still looking at the calendar.

I turned my back to him, concentrating. The phone kept ringing.

Mother walked into the room. "Excuse me, James," she said, sliding past me to open the refrigerator door. "Who are you calling, anyway?"

The phone kept ringing. I wanted to throw it at them.

"Would you like a cup of tea, Trafford?" she said, getting out the cream. "Anybody?" Then she plugged in the kettle. "This won't disturb you, will it James?" she asked.

I lost track of how many rings there had been. Twenty? But nobody was answering. Five more rings. Grandfather flipped up a page on the calendar and studied August intently, as if it was the only picture of wheatfields he'd ever seen. The kettle got louder and louder. Mother took forever finding a mug.

"Hello?" someone said, just as I hung up.

"Nobody home?" Mother said. The kettle kept boiling. Grandfather turned to look at me.

I picked up the receiver and dialled again. Her father picked up the phone immediately. "Hello Mr. Lewis sir, it's James Kinnell sir, I believe we met at Mirele's birthday party. How are you sir? Yes, I'm fine, thank you sir. I was wondering if I might have a word with Mirele sir, if she is available?" I broadcast her name loud and clear, for the benefit of all listeners in the kitchen.

"Ah — I didn't realize that sir. Well, I won't take up any more of your time. Thank you very much. Please give my regards to the missus." I slammed the receiver down, rattled.

The missus! Did I say that? *Please give my regards to the missus!*

Mother and Grandfather were both looking on, begging for information.

"What's an equestrian camp?" I asked, point blank.

"Horse riding," Mother said. The kitchen was filling up with steam from the kettle.

"Well, she's riding horses in France!" I said, and ran upstairs and laced on my running shoes and fled.

She wouldn't be back until August the fifth, which gave me just enough time to whip myself into extraordinary physical condition, if I could ever get over the embarrassment of having said to her father, "*Please give my regards to the missus.*"

When I got back, Mother and Grandfather were both oddly quiet in the living room. Grandfather exchanged glances with Mother, then followed me upstairs.

"How, uh, — *hhhrunngh!*" he said, clearing his throat. "How are things, anyway, James?"

"Fine."

"Ah," he said, nodding his head, and I got up and had a shower. When I came back he was still standing in my room.

"Is there anything — anything at all, lad, you'd like to talk about?" he asked as I towelled off.

I didn't say anything.

"Anything," he said, clearing his throat again and looking away, his face horribly red. "That you would have — *uhghghh*, asked your father about, for instance? He's not here now, you see," he said, by way of explanation.

"I think I'm fine," I said.

"I know . . . I'm not your father," he said, clearing his throat again. "At any rate, I'm here," he said, turning to leave.

"Maybe you could tell me," I said, "when I'm going to start getting hair under my arms. I mean . . . there's a little bit . . . down there, and I have some on my legs. Is there, like — an order of events? When do you think I'm going to start shaving?"

He stopped in the door. "To tell you the truth, James," he said, "I don't really remember," and then he walked down the stairs.

He came up again a few minutes later. "It's going to be a while, probably longer than you think. That's what I remember. You have to be patient."

A few days later Mother said, "If there's anything, you know, James . . . well, you're such a quiet boy, I worry sometimes. We can talk about things, you know. If there's anything —"

Talking was not our family's strong suit, so I was amazed she would even bring it up. I said, "Well, now that you mention it —" and her eyes lit up. "Are you going to marry Lee?"

She grew so red I stopped talking.

"You said I could ask," I said.

"I meant about you," she said.

"Oh."

It was as if I had stumbled into her bedroom at the wrong time. Not that she used it much anymore.

"I'm okay, I think," I said.

"Well, good," she said, nodding her head. "I know that you and Trafford . . . had a chat." She was studying the toes of her slippers. "Anyway, would you like some tea?"

We were making each other nervous, so I spent as much time as possible out of the house, going for long walks, sitting by the banks of the river and reading the most difficult books I could find so that by the time Mirele came home my mind would be as fully trained as my body. Grandfather had a *Compleat Works of Shakespeare* with print so small it was clearly meant to be just read the once and memorized as you went along. I usually had no idea what was going on but the words sounded impressive.

> *Let the bloat king tempt you again to bed;*
> *Pinch wanton on your cheek; call you his mouse;*
> *And let him, for a pair of reechy kisses,*
> *Or paddling in your neck with his damn'd fingers,*
> *Make you to ravel all this matter out,*
> *That I essentially am not in madness,*
> *But mad in craft.*

What could it mean? I didn't know, except that it had a lot to do with sex, and so mysterious that adults wanted to keep it for themselves.

One evening Mother said to me in the kitchen, "I would like . . . I was just . . . I'm worried about your grandfather. Somehow I just . . . I'm not sure that he would approve. Do you know? I need some way —"

"Approve of what?"

"Of Lee and me. I'd like to see us be . . . I'd like, well, things to be more normal."

She was looking at her slippers again and I could see that whatever she was trying to say it was just as difficult for her as the telephone call I couldn't make.

"You know it's normal . . . when two people . . . are in love," she said, "to . . . well, to sleep together. But I wanted to . . . make it easier for Trafford, and for . . . well, for all of us. I thought we could . . . well, do something together. I was thinking . . . why are you looking at me like that, James?"

I didn't know how I was looking at her.

"Would you like to go on a fishing trip?" she said, finally.

"Sure," I said.

"Well, good," she said, and we stood in silence.

"I would marry him," she said finally. "But he's still married himself."

"Lee is married?"

She nodded.

"It's not very happy. They're separated. It just takes . . . time to work things out. We have to wait sometimes."

"You're going out with a married man?"

"You're going to have to help me with Trafford on this. I know he won't . . . you're looking at me that way again," she said. "Your father used to get a look like that. You're so bloody moral, James, I hope you get away from it. It gets complicated sometimes."

"Did he separate because of you?" I asked. It hadn't occurred to me before the words left my throat. But she was hugging me for my support before I knew what to do.

"Someday it's all going to make sense," she said, and when she left that evening in tears Grandfather stood in the hallway asking me what was going on.

I shrugged.

Later I called Mirele. Of course I should never have worried about what to say to her — a simple hello was usually enough to bring down the landslide of whatever she was thinking about. We talked until my ear was sore from pressing against the receiver and my shoulder ached and my neck was stiff and Mirele's father ordered her off the phone. I lay in bed and listened as Mirele's voice chased my thoughts. To have your mother confide she has been sleeping with a married man, and then to talk about it with a beautiful girl on the telephone — well, it felt like everything had changed as quick as shadows, like I'd walked through a door and something dark and strange was ahead. When I woke up the next morning I was still thirteen and everything looked the same, but it felt different, like something a teacher had told us, how every few million years the magnetic poles would simply reverse — my north was now south, and my head was now spinning in a different way.

Grandfather knew. But he just nodded a bit and handed me a dumbbell to let me know that the important things remain — exercise, breakfast, the rest of life — reversed polarities notwithstanding.

SIX

Grandfather's older brother, Simon, arrived unannounced two days before the fishing trip. He was short and wiry and nearly bald, but he had Grandfather's hooked nose and penetrating eyes, and he carried himself as if he owned the place, wherever the place happened to be. He said, "I was in town so I thought I'd see how the family was," then he reached up to ruffle Grandfather's hair and say, "How's Daffy doing?"

"Who?" I said.

"Daffy Taffy!" Simon said, dropping a suitcase that weighed half again as much as the one Grandfather had arrived with. "You must be what's-his-name," he said to me. "I'm your Grand Uncle Simon. Where's your Mom?"

She was downstairs but came up to see what the commotion was about.

"They told me you were beautiful in your grief," he said, sweeping low with a bow. "I hope this isn't too sudden, my dear. I'm just on my way through."

Mother kissed him on the cheek. "We're leaving in a couple of days anyway," she said. "We're going on a fishing trip."

"Fishing!" Simon said. "Great thunder, it's been weeks since I've been fishing."

"Why don't you come with us?" Mother asked, even though Grandfather was gesturing *No!* behind Simon's back. "But you said you were on your way somewhere else . . ."

"Nothing that can't wait for fishing," Simon said, breaking into a big smile.

Simon slept on the couch that night, and when I got up early the next morning to do my exercises with Grandfather it was too late; the brothers had already paced one another through an entire routine and were now headed out the door for a marathon walk before breakfast.

Mother had not slept well. She was worried because she had not yet told Grandfather that Lee was coming on the trip. She had meant to tell him several days before — the whole purpose of the trip was so that Lee could join the family publicly and . . . well, so that she and Lee could sleep together and Grandfather would accept it instead of pretending it wasn't happening. They couldn't get married; Lee's divorce was going to take awhile, but they wanted to "come out" anyway.

She said, "It's going to be even harder with Simon here. When am I going to get Trafford alone?"

"Why does he have to be so hidebound?" she said, shuffling about the kitchen in a pre-breakfast daze. "And why should I care what he thinks? But you know what he's going to say —"

"Mom —"

"'They're *shacking up!*' He'll say it just like that — 'In my day, we used to call it *shacking up!*'"

"Mom, do you mind if I bring a friend along?"

"He'll say — 'Of course it doesn't bother me. Why should it bother me — you're just *shacking up!*'" She gulped down a steadying dose of grapefruit juice. "What was that, dear?"

"Could I bring a friend on the fishing trip?"

"I don't see why not," she said, staring into her glass. "*Shacking up!*" she said, pulling her hand through her hair.

I should have told Mother the truth, that the friend I'd already asked to come along was Mirele. Mother just assumed it was going to be a boy, an impression I failed to correct, just as Grandfather assumed that Lee was not coming, an impression that Mother failed to correct. Lee showed up before sunrise as we were preparing our luggage. He had a huge knapsack on his back and six different fishing rods snuggled in his arms. I thought for a moment Grandfather was going to hit him.

"Boy, I've been looking forward to this all week!" Lee said as he came in. "Good morning, Trafford, how are you doing?"

Grandfather cleared his throat, nodded, and carried on without a word.

"What's this — a gentleman caller?" Simon said, thrusting his hand forward, and the two men shook hands. "God you've got a firm grip, boy!"

Grandfather proceeded to pack the car, brushing off aid by claiming the superior knowledge of a marine engineer. "We've got enough gear here to outfit the entire Chinese army," he muttered. "You people sit down and finish your coffee. I'm going to have to put this together scientifically."

Simon and Mother and Lee went back into the kitchen, but I stayed out by the car handing things to Grandfather and nervously scanning the road. Mirele was already late; it would be just like her to sleep in or forget entirely that she said she would come.

Grandfather finished the packing, stepped back to survey a trunk that couldn't hold an extra molecule of luggage. The others came out and Mother said, "James, didn't you say you had a friend who was going to —"

Then there she was, walking down the road in a summer dress splashed with East Indian colours and a big straw hat, carrying two suitcases and a knapsack. The sun was rising behind her, the breeze wrapped the skirt of her dress around her body, and I could barely move, she was so beautiful.

"I'm sorry I'm late," she said, walking up to me and kissing me partly on the cheek — but mostly on the lips. She put down her bags. "Hello, Mrs. Kinnell," she said, putting out her hand. "I've heard so much about you. I'm Mirele. And you must be Lee," she said. She picked out Grandfather too — "You're so tall!" — while Mother looked on stunned and I nearly exploded with pride.

"I will *not* tie a trunk shut!" Grandfather proclaimed a little later, and so we were another half hour while he took everything out and repacked. I think he was trying to im-press Mirele. She stayed with him and they talked about Scotland and Australia and Hong Kong. "Of course I haven't been back to Hong Kong in many years," Grandfather said. "But in my day you could walk into a restaurant in Kowloon and they could wipe your table, take your order, serve you, bring dessert and have your bill in about seven minutes, all without your feeling you were being rushed. They snapped to it. No time to waste, those Chinese. The whole colony re-minded me of an anthill."

"A very *rich* anthill, now," Mirele said, and when he finally got all the bags in she touched his arm — I noted the gesture.

"Now where did James ever find you?" he said, his face glowing.

Grandfather insisted on driving. And both he and Simon insisted that Mirele sit up front, between them. I stayed in the back beside Mother, who leaned against Lee like some teenager in love — exactly the way Mirele and I should have been sitting, because we, after all, were the teenagers. But Mirele and Simon and Grandfather, for some reason, rattled on about ancient Greece. "A great many people forget," Grandfather said, "that Aristotle was the teacher of Alexan-der the Great. Not only have his works lived on in history, but his teachings directly inspired —" and Simon said, "What do you think of Greek men, Mirele? Are they all they're cracked up to be?"

"Well, they're not all Aristotle and Alexander," Mirele said. "I think Aristotle was far too conservative for my tastes. He would be a very intimidating teacher. And Alexander — well, you'd never see him, would you? There would always be something else to conquer . . . "

It was galling to observe, the two of them falling all over themselves — and each other — for the girl *I* had invited, who was charming them with the ease of flipping pancakes. The city in August sped by the window and turned into fields and bush and rockcuts for mile after mile as we drove north. I should never have invited her, I thought. It was all a mistake.

Grandfather was a nervous driver. Both hands perpetually on the wheel, he hunched his body forward and scanned the road so vigilantly it seemed certain that disasters would lurch out at us. With such a dangerous world out there, there was no point even approaching the speed limit, so long lines of traffic formed behind us, with one or two cars flinging themselves past us every time there was an empty straight stretch and occasionally around bends, life itself apparently having lost much of its value if it had to be lived stuck behind a slowpoke. Every time we felt the wind of a passing vehicle it was like a vote of non-confidence for Grandfather who would refuse to turn his head to see who the fool was in such a hurry, although he would slow down to help the person by, thus angering the line behind him.

"You drive like an old woman!" Simon said, reaching across Mirele to get to the steering wheel as if he could snatch it away and steer on his side for awhile. Grandfather fended him off while Mirele squirmed between them and the car slowed even more. I'm not sure what bothered me more, the fact that my life was being threatened or my girlfriend was being sandwiched in front of me.

Actually, I was all too aware that Mirele was not my girlfriend, a state of affairs I wished to remedy during this fishing trip. It seemed clear to me that she would be — why else had she agreed to go? It would just be a matter of being alone somewhere, with the lap of the water and a gentle breeze, and I would ask her, and when she said yes I would give her the gift I had bought, a tiny heart pendant with a pearl inside on a gold chain. I would say, "You are like a pearl in my heart," and it would be very romantic, and then . . .

Mist Lake Lodge was a collection of six cabins stuck in the woods, all painted the same faded mouldy green. No visible renovations had been made in about forty years. As a result the wooden steps had a soggy, dangerous spring to them, the screen doors had no spring at all, and the beds were all sag, as were the roofs, and all the furniture inside smelled as if it had been soaking for some decades in cigar smoke and alcohol.

But the lake was magical, so calm it reflected the sky in a silver mirror, the stillness broken only by the sudden flight of a rainbow trout launching itself into the air. It was extraordinary to see — *there! another one!* — *two more at the edge of the bay* — and we rushed to the water, the bother of the trip falling from us. In a moment Grandfather and Simon had filled a rental boat with Lee's gear, and the two experienced fishermen had launched themselves — with Mirele — while Mother and Lee and I looked on. Mirele didn't even look back. Simon was leaning over her explaining something, while Grandfather wrestled with the motor and trout jumped all around.

Mother didn't really want to go fishing, so I spent the afternoon in a second rental boat with Lee. It was my first time alone with him. I suppose Mother had imagined that we would "bond" somehow, sitting in the same boat, especially if we shared the age-old triumph of bringing dinner wriggling to our feet. But we hadn't quite got our lures in the water when clouds closed in and it began to rain, a steady cold downpour that drove away all the fish. We sat through it glumly without rain gear, neither of us wishing to be the first to quit.

Lee couldn't seem to think of a thing to say, and I certainly wasn't going to help him. "So, you're still married and you're sleeping with my mother?" is the phrase that ran over and over in my head, and I couldn't say that, so I kept quiet and watched the rain.

"You're going into grade seven, is that right?" he asked at one point.

"Nine," I said.

"Ah," he said, not quite looking at me.

I could see Mirele, Grandfather and Simon in the distance. Mirele was wearing Simon's sweater and holding a fishing rod and the three of them bantered for much of the afternoon, the laughter, if not the actual words, drifting across the water. Simon seemed to be reeling in a fish every time I looked in their direction; he was loud and boisterous with every triumph, while Grandfather's stentorian *shhhhhs!* echoed across the lake and Mirele pointed and laughed and struggled with the net.

Lee said, "Maybe we should go over there. That seems to be where all the fish are."

I said, "No, let's stay here."

And the afternoon drained away.

When I was thoroughly soaked and cold and miserable, Simon and Grandfather and Mirele finally headed back in which meant that we could as well, except that Lee had a hard time starting the motor. He pulled and pulled at the cord, until finally he said, "I must have flooded it," and so we waited awhile longer. I stared morosely into the water.

Lee said, "Maybe people won't tell you, but you've got a hard way of looking, James."

"What?"

"Your face," he said. "It comes directly from your grandfather — a very fierce expression. I don't think you realize you're even doing it. Like right now. You're looking at me so hard it seems like you want to strip the skin from my bone. I just flooded the engine. It's not so bad. We'll be all right in a minute."

I didn't say anything. He said, "Whatever you think of me, your mother needs someone. You'll know that someday. Being all alone . . . gets harder when you get older." He tried the motor again. Still nothing.

"So, you're still married and you're sleeping with my mother, is that it?" I said.

"I am loving your mother," he said quietly, and I couldn't think of a single thing to say. I don't think he could either. The motor started the next pull and we went in.

We had rented two cabins. In Mother's original plan, I realized, she and Lee were to stay in one and Grandfather and I were to stay in the other. Simon too would stay with us, but the advent of Mirele suddenly changed everything. Now the women were in one cabin and the men in the other, but if Mother was disappointed about the arrangements she didn't show it. When our boat pulled in she had a towel ready for me and a questioning look for Lee — "Did you speak to him?" she seemed to be asking; "Yes — later," Lee seemed to reply.

We ate Simon's fish for dinner, cooked in the "girls'" cabin. Simon and Grandfather had a terrible argument over fishing techniques. Grandfather was a fly fisherman at heart and even clipped the barbs off his hooks to be more sporting while Simon committed the unspeakable sin of using live bait. The two went on and on, kidding and deadly serious at the same time. They looked like they were going to come to blows.

That was when I left. I brushed past them and walked out to the shore where I crouched on a flat rock. It was still raining. The clouds were so low now they seemed to be pressing

against the lake. It was almost dark, and I felt an unspeakable rage inside, fuelled by everything that was happening,
the whole convoluted situation . . . but it was also my age, not
old enough yet, not a real person, not an adult, whatever an
adult was.

The knots doubled and tripled inside me while the rain
came down and the sounds of bitter arguments splintered
from the cabin. I somehow expected Mirele to leave them
too; to come out and talk with me, and that would be our
peaceful moment. I had the pendant right in my pocket.
Everything would be perfect. I would say, "You are like a
pearl in my heart," and then —

I waited. I got soaked again. She didn't come.

And so I went back to the "boys'" cabin, changed in the
dark and slipped into the farthest of the two double beds.
Somebody was going to have to share it with me; I didn't
want to think about who it would be. I wanted to be asleep
when they came in, safely alone in another world.

When the others came in Grandfather and Simon argued
about whether or not they should turn on the light — "*Shhh!*"
said Grandfather, and "He's okay, he's asleep!" said Simon,
and I felt them peering over me. My eyes were closed and I
tried to relax my breathing. Someone lit a gas lamp on the
other side of the room. "Boy, it's been a long day," said Lee,
yawning. "It's still early yet," said Simon. "I am not playing
cards with you," said Grandfather.

"Just a hand or two," said Simon. "Lee looks like a real
card player."

"I'm pretty tired," said Lee.

"Absolutely not," said Grandfather.

They played for three hours.

I don't remember what started it, but they'd been fighting all day anyway, so it was no surprise that as time went on

voices got louder and the play became secondary. They started talking about family. They were drinking some kind of rum that Simon had brought.

"Lee, my good man," Simon said at one point. "I've never seen anyone *moon* over a woman in quite the way of our Daffy here. She was delightful, it was true. He should have married her. Why didn't you marry her? You see, look at his face now. I haven't even said her name and he's ready to kill me. He *never* got over it. *Six decades later* he never —"

"You've no right to talk about Colleen," Grandfather said. "She refused me and she —"

"Died, right. Yes. We all know the story. It happened a hell of a long time ago. We've fought world wars since then. We've gone to the moon and back."

"You have never loved a woman," Grandfather said.

"I've loved so many women I can't keep track of them all!" Simon said. "Most importantly my wife. I didn't suffer through forty years of steadfast bitterness with some woman I hated so much I ran off to sea every chance —"

"You will not speak of Dorothy in that —"

"Oh, sit down, Daffy. You know what your problem is? Your problem —" And they were both standing now. "Hey! Hey!" Lee said, coming between them.

"Your problem," Simon said, "is that everything sticks to you. Nothing slides off. Relax for God's sakes! Let it go!"

"You have never let a true sentiment penetrate your stainless steel —"

"Shrug your shoulders! They're big enough! Move on! She died for Christ sakes!"

"Come on, young Daffy!" Simon taunted. "You've been wanting this for years and years. Take your best shot. You've —"

Grandfather cocked his fist. "No!" I shouted, springing out of bed. Anybody would have, if they'd seen like I had the

73

thunderous way that Grandfather pounded the heavy bag in our basement. They both looked at me. Grandfather put down his fist.

"I wasn't going to hit him," he said in a little voice.

"Of course not," Simon said. "I'd break his arm. He knows that. I'm his big brother."

I looked from the tiny man to the giant. They both started laughing.

"Egad," Grandfather said. "It must be time for bed."

I had the misfortune of sleeping with Grandfather. It was like being moored beside the Titanic, his snores reverberating like foghorn blasts. Every so often his whole body would twitch in a spasm and he would groan half-words, snorting out some argument, before subsiding again for a few minutes. I finally did fall asleep, but only when I was exhausted.

When I woke up it was light and the three men were gone fishing. I staggered to the outhouse and then over to the "girls'" cabin where the smell of bacon and eggs went a long way to wiping out the disastrous night. Mother and Mirele looked like sisters, rumple-haired and sleepy-eyed and sharing secret glances about whatever it was they'd been talking of the night before. Mirele was wearing Mother's big green sweater. "How did you sleep?" she asked and I told them all about it over breakfast.

"Your Mother's a really neat person," Mirele said to me later, when we were behind the cabin at the woodpile. I was chopping kindling, swinging the big axe, trying to look like I knew what I was doing without cutting off my foot. "She's very warm," Mirele said. "My mother's an iceberg compared to her. We talked most of the night. It was like a sleep-over or something."

"What did you talk about?" I asked, setting up a spindly log that was sure to split easily. I raised the axe above my head, and then brought it down about a yard wide, burying it in the soft ground.

"Well, about Lee's children for one," she said.

"His *what*?"

"He's got kids. Three of them. Two, six, and eight. He's, like, torn apart by this whole thing."

"You mean by *his* whole thing. He made it."

"It's love," Mirele said. "It's messy a lot of the time. It doesn't follow rules."

I brought the axe down again and split the log like Abe Lincoln, then turned to see the look in her eyes, whether her falling for a thirteen-year-old boy was possible in this messy world.

If it was she wasn't letting on. She was looking at her boots with her arms folded across Mother's green sweater. "Your Grandfather and Simon are just a scream," she said. "I can imagine them running around in short pants being sibling rivals all over the place. It's kind of sweet. My brother and I — we don't even intersect most of the time. He's in a different universe."

"I wouldn't know," I said. "I don't have a sibling."

"Oh, yes you do," she said. "Your mother made me an honorary member of the family last night. I'm like your sister now."

I don't think I said anything. She was smiling, and the sun was behind her and there was the smell of the lake and the pine needles. But my heart was sinking. The pendant stayed in my pocket. The movie part of my brain prompted the line, "Well, if you're my sister I should give you a kiss," and commanded me to stride over to her and take her in my arms in a most unbrotherly fashion.

I didn't move.

"I guess that's enough wood," she said, bending over to pick up the pieces.

"The thing about love is you want to stay a little cool," Simon said to me. We were in the boat late in the afternoon. We were out alone and every time he put his line in the water he seemed to be getting a bite, while I was getting absolutely nothing no matter what I did.

"You want to hang back a little if you can," he said. "Try to keep from riding straight off the cliff. It's not so impressive to girls."

I nodded. He said, "I think you've got the defective gene that runs in our family. God knows Daffy has it. Whatever it is, he falls so hard he's like this great oak with no roots. A little puff of wind and he's flat on his face. He'd have had his Colleen if he'd hung back a bit."

I just looked at him.

"I know you're a young snapper, but I can see the way you look at Mirele. She's very fine, all right. But you'd better hang back a bit." He paused. "I said the same thing to your Grandfather about sixty years ago. God, it's a funny life. Let's go in."

It wasn't a long trip. I never got Mirele alone again — she was always surrounded by the brothers or talking to my mother. Lee and Mother didn't get much time together either. Grandfather was ubiquitous, forever looking at them in his way, and so they didn't hold hands on the dock or go off together in the boat, much less sleep together. After Mirele's explanation it seemed to me Lee was a man with something missing, with something on his mind — with kids at home who needed him. Like he'd ridden straight off the cliff and wasn't quite sure where to go next, except down.

He was the one who drove us back — in a hurry, passing long lines of traffic through a thick rain while Mother endured. I sat between them. They'd had a fight which was still silently raging. "It's going to be slow, Lee," Mother said at one point. "You don't have to pass all these people. We'll get there."

Lee didn't comment, didn't even look at her.

Mirele sat in the back, gazing out the window. Grandfather and Simon were slumped together, snoring, Grandfather's arm around his brother's shoulder. They would have made a good photograph. All in all it seemed to me we were a perfect portrait of a woeful family with windows up against the rain, huddled and angry and loving and alone, thinking our own thoughts, hurtling along but seemingly going nowhere, together.

Then at the end of the trip everything fell apart. Grandfather was pulling the bags out of the trunk; Mother and Lee were not speaking; Simon was stretching himself awake, as if wondering what life this was. Grandfather said to Mirele, "It's been a real pleasure, young lass. I hope we see lots of you in the coming days." And she ducked her head a little bit, looking at Grandfather but looking at me too, out of the corner of her eye.

"I'd like to, yes," she said, brushing some hair out of her face. "But I'm afraid my father's gone back to the foreign service. We're going to Jakarta for four years. It's supposed to be dreadfully polluted. I hardly want to think about it, actually." She turned to me. "But we're family now anyway," she said. "Honorary siblings. So —"

Whatever else was said, I didn't hear it. There was just the rush of the wind, and the way the world looks, spinning so, when the road has turned into cliff and you've ridden straight off.

SEVEN

Mirele was gone within two weeks. She said, on our last walk together, which we took along the river where my father proposed to my mother, "I meant to tell you. But it's hard sometimes. Especially the way you look — it's like, you get this dreadfully flammy expression, I don't know what it is, like you're a Puritanical avenger or something. I know you're very gentle inside. But the way you look sometimes."

She also said, "I really am an awful letter writer, so I'll apologize right now. You could still write me, though. I bet you'd be good. You're so patient. I'll send you my address."

It came seven months later, written in tiny letters in the corner of a post card showing a huge pile of ruins nearly overgrown by forest. "It's so mouldy here your feet start to take root if you stay still too long. School has been drastic. I'll write you a real letter shortly."

I waited for three weeks, then wrote her a letter of my own, and waited four more weeks, and wrote again, and then waited three more months before her second card arrived, showing palm trees and pure ocean and white sand. "Bali. My father nearly died of sunstroke today — darling Mummy let him fall asleep on the beach at noon and then walked away from him because he was drunk. Don't be surprised if they murder each other. The European girls on the beach next door are all bare-chested — you'd be in heaven here. Got to go!" And then in microscopic script in one corner, "Any girlfriends yet?"

The card made me so angry I refused to write for another month, but then Lee and Mother broke up, so I had to tell her about that. Everything had been going along as it always had — Mother staying at Lee's workshop a few nights a week, Lee rarely showing his face at our house, Grandfather grumbling in the background. But there were no more fishing trips; Mother didn't talk any more about getting us all together as a "family." Then one supper Mother stood up at the table so abruptly she nearly knocked over her wine glass. She said, "I'm only going to say this once. Lee's wife is having another baby. By Lee. You were both absolutely, bloody well right. And if anyone says another word about it at any time, I'll scream."

She stared us both down, then went up to her room and slammed the door.

Grandfather didn't move.

I said, "I should go talk to her."

He said, "That's not a good idea, lad."

I started to get up. He put a heavy hand on my arm. "Some things," he said, "you just leave alone. Sit down."

He continued eating. I took his hand off my arm. I went up the stairs and stood outside her door, listening. I couldn't even hear her breathing. I put my hand on the knob and turned the handle. I pushed it open a crack.

She was sitting on the edge of the bed, naked. Her clothes were scattered about the room as if a wild wind had blown them off her body. She had a mirror in her hand. She was running her other hand through her hair. Her face looked more streaked with rain than tears.

I closed the door and went back downstairs.

And so we didn't talk about Lee.

I wrote to Mirele instead, of how the air in our house was charged with electricity, and you couldn't be sure when Mother was going to burst into tears. There was a letter from Lee which she tore up and threw in the garbage without opening, and he came once to the door but Grandfather wouldn't let him in. He phoned several times. When I answered I told him that Mother was out; when Grandfather answered he lectured him on morality and family duties; and the one time Mother answered she shrieked directly into the phone. I don't think he called again after that.

I continued my running, my morning workouts, my boxing with Grandfather after school. I grew about four inches the year I was fifteen. I entirely lost whatever ability I had to talk to girls. I don't know what it was about Mirele, but talking to her was like sliding down an icy slope on a toboggan. But with girls at school words caught like fishhooks in the back of my throat; my face flamed and I couldn't bring my eyes above the tips of my own shoes. Everyone seemed older than me, even the ones who were younger, and it was easier to be silent, to run hard and read and wait.

Mother spent a lot of time in her room. Grandfather played the violin for her. It was as if, like Father, Lee too had died, and our house was filled with the particular sadness that Grandfather had nurtured much of his life. I wrote to Mirele nearly daily, a kind of journal of what I considered my prison notes — the thoughts of a person condemned to adolescence, to looking through barred windows at Life, at adulthood, at the world outside.

I sent letter after letter. Nothing came back. I turned sixteen and stopped writing, although I was still in prison, my body becoming more and more charged with a sexuality I had no idea what to do with — or rather, how to cope with. I was rigid at night when I went to bed and rigid in the morning when I sat at the breakfast table, rigid at the oddest times in class. Rigid when reading; rigid when looking out the window; rigid in the middle of a math problem when a curve becomes a breast and a line a lock of hair and a triangle, a simple triangle, becomes the intersection of great longings that disappear into black mystery.

I was a basket-case, locked in prison with the world erupting inside me *and no one to tell it to*, no one to confide in. Not Mother, whose image while naked that day burned in my brain; not Grandfather, whose specialty was things not talked about, whose life stood for discipline and strength and silence. I'd fallen directly into the hole in the kitchen floor, and its vow too was one of silence. Never mind the time I spent erupting silently in the bathroom, in the bedroom, in the basement with the lights off and the feel of gritty floor between my toes. Never mind the semen-soaked wads of paper that offered temporary relief along with their promise of madness and addiction — who have I become? What is this sickness? The outer part of my life is still the same — I still walk to school, do my homework, eat dinner with Mother and Grandfather, and we find things to say to each other . . .

Is this it, being grown-up? Being a physical addict, spilling my seed in private with scenes of imagined women taking over my brain? Somehow I thought it would be more noble than this.

The miracle that happened at this stage, the one great thing that finally went right, for a while, was that Mirele came back, showed up at our door nearly three years to the day after she left. She was barefoot, with a knapsack across her shoulders and a huge white sunhat tilted on her head, the kind that Asian women in pictures wear in rice paddies.

"Hello, James," she said and I just stood there holding the door. It wouldn't have surprised me if I'd lost my brain to visions of women; I'd been losing the battle for quite a while by then and was near surrender anyway.

But she was real.

"Did you get my letter?" she asked, stepping in. "No," I said, unsure whether to hug her or hit her.

"There wasn't a lot of time," she said. "I guess maybe it'll come in a few days. Here, I've got to put this down or I'll break my back." She slid the straps off her shoulders and eased the pack to the floor.

She was a little slenderer, perhaps, her hair looked wilder, and her skin was quite brown. She was significantly shorter too — we'd been nearly even three years before, and now I was almost a head taller.

"Things kind of crashed at home," she said. "I was hoping I could stay with you for a bit."

"For how long?" I asked.

"A year maybe. If that's all right?"

It was all right. Eventually. It took a lot of explaining, especially since Mirele was not very forthcoming with details. She painted a picture of an alcoholic father, a desperately unhappy mother, and an American school in Jakarta which she just could not adjust to and so she lost her year. She still needed five credits before she could graduate from high school. She wanted to live with us and go back to her old school to do it.

The letter she said was on the way never came. She didn't mention it again.

But Grandfather immediately began to renovate the basement, he was so excited at the prospect of having Mirele at home. The punching bags he had erected for us the week of his own arrival were dumped in the corner near the furnace. Life at home had been too gloomy even for Grandfather since the breakup. It was Mother who was reluctant, though she refused to say why. But when Mirele finally got a letter from her parents giving their permission there was no reason to refuse.

"You did make me an honorary member of the family, after all," Mirele said.

The basement provided no five-star accommodations, despite Grandfather's and my best efforts. It was still dark and mouldy and damp, no place for a guest, so I offered my own bedroom to Mirele. At first she refused but eventually we switched, and I settled into my cave just as we settled into a new routine. During the day we walked to school, and she flirted with Grandfather while making the dinner and sewed and talked with Mother in the early evening, and sometimes, late at night, when all the lights were off and the house was rocking gently to sounds of Grandfather's snoring, she crept down to my room and set me ablaze.

I can't remember when it first happened — perhaps October; it was cool at night but the furnace was not yet on. I was asleep and thought she was an extension of my dream, sliding into bed beside me. "What are you wearing clothes for?" she said, shaking my shoulder.

"These aren't clothes," I said, going along with the dream. "These are pyjamas."

"A boy your age should not be sleeping in pyjamas," she said. The bottoms were off in one smooth movement, and I was awake. She pulled so hard on the top that the buttons flew off.

Then she laughed with her head thrown back, like we were all alone in the desert with only the stars to hear us.

"What, are you crazy?" I said, putting my hand over her mouth. "Yes," she said, and bit my finger, not gently either, and laughed even louder, and then pressed against me with her lithe, warm, naked body, those nipples I had dreamed about alert in the cool air.

In less than a minute I was spurting all over her.

"There," she said, mopping me up with a washcloth from the shower. "Some lover you are. You didn't even kiss me and you've already come." The tone in her voice made me feel ashamed, yet she was smiling, her face glorious and alive.

"Don't come to me," she said, kissing me lightly as she left. "And don't wear pyjamas to bed anymore."

The next morning at breakfast she was radiant, and she and Grandfather talked about whether Shakespeare really knew anything about women at all. "All his women were men in drag," she said, her eyes sparkling. "Or they went mad. Or both." And while Grandfather quoted his collected works she let her eyes swim over me across the table.

On the way to school we talked about algebra and school politics and my training for the cross-country running team. I tried to hold her hand but she hissed, "*I will come to you!*"

I didn't wear pyjamas that night. The instant my head hit the pillow I heard something crinkling and found a note in her wild script. *Don't touch yourself*, it said. I waited, eyes open, listening for her soft tread down the stairs, imagining her cool skin, the rich smell of her hair, the wildness of her laugh. First thing, when she arrived, I would kiss her. We would just spend the whole night kissing. And then I would tell her that I was going to marry her — that I'd always known it.

But she didn't come. I was still rigid at breakfast. On the walk to school we talked about environmental disasters threatening the earth.

I waited the next night, and the next. It was a long wait.

Nearly three weeks. I was asleep when she came again. "Did you touch yourself?" she asked, nudging me awake.

"No."

"Good."

That was as far as we got for talking. Her kisses raced liked white water, her breathing was frantic and driven, until it felt like I was sharing my bed with a wild presence half-seen in darkness. She was on top of me and we rolled off the mattress, against the wall, then back onto the mattress. I was pinned and she grabbed my shoulders, thrusting her hips against me, and then we rolled again and she pulled me inside her. I was shocked, alarmed, almost frightened — rivetted and aroused and yet strangely apart, as if watching an accident from inside the car but not believing it was happening. She screamed suddenly, loud enough to echo through the vents, and I was sure that Mother and Grandfather both were going to materialize at the bottom of the stairs.

She didn't return for five weeks. It was nearly winter by then, and our big oil furnace was roaring into life every half hour throughout the night. I'd almost given up on sleep — she was on my mind constantly. I tried to kiss her once in the hallway when Mother and Grandfather were both upstairs; she turned her face as if I were a porcupine.

"You were doing so well," she said, and walked past, leaving me pale and breathless with remorse.

"What is it?" I asked on our walk to school. "Why can't we talk about it? Why can't we be open, at least with each other? It's the thing I hate about my whole family, we never talk about anything!"

"This isn't for talking," she hissed.

"I want to marry you," I said.

"Oh well," she said, looking for all the world as if something else was going to follow, but it didn't.

She got lots of mail, most of it from her parents, but usually a few other pieces each week from overseas. She didn't seem to write very much herself, although she did spend quite a bit of time alone in her room, her schoolbooks open, pen in hand. One Saturday afternoon when she and Grandfather were shopping and Mother was working overtime at the office I went through Mirele's things, looking for her letters. Who were they from? Other lovers left breathless, longing, adrift? Boyfriends on every continent? I slammed the drawers open and shut.

Nothing. She didn't keep the letters. I wondered if she even read them.

When she came into my room again it was after Christmas and I wasn't so cooperative. "This is driving me nuts," I said.

"Shhh."

"Who do you think you are? Do you think you can just order me around? You're not making love to me, you're power-tripping. Even I can see that. Here —"

She slapped my face so hard I hit the bed, and when I looked up she was disappearing up the stairs.

"Hey! Wait! Hey!" I said, catching her arm and twirling her around. "Don't just walk away from me. Who do you think I am?"

"Well who do you think *I* am?" she asked.

I didn't have an answer. She said, "I'll come back when you've found your manners."

It took several more weeks. I apologized to her daily. I wrote her long letters. I begged her to come. I told her I would do anything she wanted. And so we started up, one or two times a week, only when she wanted. She blew in like a storm and then disappeared, leaving me beached, dismasted. I don't know what she did for birth control. We never discussed it.

The more we were lovers, the less I felt I knew her. Where was the girl who used to talk endlessly of the affairs her father was having, who used to want to know so much of what was happening at my house, who was hungering to learn about the world that happened at night behind closed doors and drawn curtains, that adults pretended wasn't there? She was a young woman now, a part of that world, charming Grandfather with her literary arguments, being a sister to my mother, kidding me in front of the family about when I was going to ask a girl out. Her act was convincing; there didn't seem to be any intersection between the honorary sister who had moved in and the frantic lover whose footstep on the stair raced my blood. Was this what being an adult was all about — schizophrenia?

One night in the early spring she came to me and my body didn't respond. I was training hard for the track season then and had a bit of a cold, but mostly it was several months of unspoken anger, confusion and resentment. What was this about? Practice? She pinned my shoulders to the bed and in the darkness I could just make out the fear in her eyes. There wasn't a word I could think of to say that wouldn't come out wounding.

She didn't speak to me for days. Even Mother and Grandfather noticed. Mother said to me, "Is she all right? Did you two have a fight? Is there anything you want to talk about?"

I shook my head.

Grandfather came into my room when I was studying. "Your — uh, your mother asked me to talk to you."

I looked at him from the chair at my desk.

"We were just wondering if there's anything —"

"No," I said.

"You're growing up so fast," he said. "There's going to be some . . . feelings happening soon." He cleared his throat. "If you want to talk about them —"

Yes, I did. But I couldn't say a word.

"Well, you know where I am," he said, having done his duty. I watched him go.

I waited for her to come to me to clear the air. She had never in her life cleared the air: not after her birthday over three years before, not when she wouldn't talk to me for those months, not when she showed up at our door so suddenly after hardly responding to all I had written. She was either not acknowledging your existence or she was ploughing through the present as if the past had never happened. This time it was up to her to come to me to find out what was wrong.

Then one night I heard her. Months of waiting had conditioned me to wake up at the sound of her steps. But they weren't coming down the stairs. They were opening the front door; disappearing down the walk. I threw on my clothes and went after her. It was cold. The snow had barely gone and we could see our breath.

"Where are you going?" I asked. She didn't put down her knapsack. She only stopped when I put a hand on her shoulder.

"You hit me and I'll scream," she said in her carving-knife voice.

"I'm not going to hit you," I said.

She looked at my hand until I took it off her, and then she started walking again. I walked along with her.

"You can't just leave," I said. "Where are you going to go? You don't have any money, do you? We have a problem here that we should talk about, that's all. I just want to talk about it."

"What's there to talk about?" she said. "You hate me."

"I don't hate you."

"Fine." She kept on walking. She said, "I thought I could do something, I could be someone to you. But it wasn't working out. So it's better this way. You'll have some nice memories of me."

"You are someone to me," I said. "I want to marry you. I've always wanted to marry you. I've never thought about anyone the way that I —"

"Oh, God," she said, stopping, the knapsack falling off her shoulders with a clump. "I hate it when guys talk like that. You're turning into a guy. I hate that."

"What do you hate?"

"You were going to be different," she said. "I could see that. You look so shy but there's a lot going on behind those eyes. You could be calm and gentle and patient. You could appreciate when something comes your way. Most guys can't. They have to be driving the bus or it's no go. I thought you weren't going to be like that. I thought —"

"You've been calling the shots ever since we met," I said. "I was happy just to be with you. I always was! But you've got to let me —"

"Oh dear," she said, and then she went up on her toes and kissed me. "This is getting drastic," she said, sighing. "I'm always going to remember you. Could you say good-bye to your mother and grandfather for me?"

There was no more discussing it. I carried her bag to the bus station. It was a mile and a half. The station was deserted; the ticket booth was closed. We sat together on the bench, waiting for the sun to come up. She fell asleep against my chest, and I was happy to just hold her, to feel her breathing, to watch her face so smooth and unreadable.

"What are you going to do about school?" I asked her when she woke up and smiled at me.

"Stay and finish," she said.

She never cleared the air, Mirele — but she had a way of turning around and there, the air was clear after all. We got back and slipped into the house while Grandfather was in the shower and Mother was still asleep. It became obvious to them though that something had changed between us. I think they assumed that we had become lovers. Nothing was said, of course, but a large package of condoms appeared in the cupboard in the bathroom. I never used them. Mirele didn't come to my bed again. Sometimes in the evenings when the weather got warmer we would go for long walks along the river and hold hands, and talk and talk the way two people do when they are meant to share a life. My heart soared with every step, and Grandfather looked at us the way he would look at spring blossoms bursting in bloom, and Mother drank her coffee not asking, holding back like someone trying not to cry at a movie.

Mirele graduated with honours in June. I still had two more years. She left a few days later to see her parents. Her plan was to travel for a bit in India and then come back in the fall to start university. She was going to live with us. She was going to bring us back an oriental rug.

Three years later we heard from her again. She sent us a card from St. Andrews, in Scotland. "It's raining again," she wrote, as if updating a long series of letters. "My programme is almost through — it's been grisly. We went to Prestwick and watched the lights at the edge of the runway at night. It was like galaxies were speeding by. Did I tell you I'm getting married? It's almost embarrassing how these things happen, isn't it? Thinking of you always — Mirele."

EIGHT

"I'm going after her," I said.

"You're not going to do anything of the like," Mother said.

"I'll take the term off. I'll use the tuition for a ticket. When we get back I can work part-time to —"

"Your father and I did not invest that money so that you could go traipsing off after —"

We argued day and night. "Why are you condemning me for doing exactly what Father did when he married you? Wasn't your life happy? He did what he had to do."

"It was different!" Mother screamed.

"It wasn't different! It's the same! It's exactly the same. It's not sleeping around with some married guy who's still sleeping with his wife too!"

It was as if the cover was ripped off and our family life had spilled out.

"Who was sleeping with whom right under my roof, sneaking around late at night, pretending to be little miss —"

"Don't speak of Mirele that way!"

"She's treated you like shit and now —"

Day and night, in circles, until we were exhausted.

"She wants me to come, it's the only reason she sent me the card. She wants me to come to her. When Mirele does something it's all by feeling, it doesn't happen step-by-step. I know her so well. I love her so much. She wants me to come and get her, that's all."

"Love isn't like this," Mother said in a little voice. "You have to be so careful with it. Because you want it so much. But there should be no gamble in it. You should know, right down absolutely in your heart. There should be no question . . . *that the other person loves you the same way*."

"She will," I said. "She does. She just . . . has a funny way of communicating it."

"She has an extremely perverse way of communicating it," Mother said. "Why can't you just trust me? She's hurt you already so much. It's not going to work out. Even if you got her, it wouldn't work out. And you're still so young."

"The same age as Father when he married you," I said.

"It's not the same," she said, over and over again.

In the end I went to Grandfather, who had stayed strangely silent throughout. "She has chosen someone else," he said at first. "That's very clear to me." When I asked him again he said, "You should finish your schooling."

"What would *you* do?" I asked him.

"I know what I *did*," he said.

"But what would you do *now*?"

"Exactly as you," he said after a pause.

I went alone, but Grandfather and Father were both with me. All the love that had been spent as young men on Colleen and on Mother I felt was in me now. How powerful to be young and strong and suddenly know which way to go, what to do. As I sat thousands of feet above the Atlantic I felt that had the engines blown away I could have flown the plane myself.

I entered in the customs line amazed at having stepped beyond the boundaries of my life. A businessman stood in front of me, bored, his grey suit rumpled, his luggage stuffed and expensive. A slender woman with the beginnings of grey hair in blonde leaned on her bags behind me with two boys wrestling one another around the edges of her skirt. In another line an elderly lady with just one small bag — a seasoned traveller, I thought — watched us all, but mostly me, I thought, reading what she could in my face.

I'm not sure now how I blundered from the airport to the train station. I remember trying to read a subway map. Was this the right line? Where would this take me? Which stop would it be? It didn't occur to me to ask people. This was something I had to do for myself, *by* myself. In the little notebook I kept as a diary I wrote, "The pursuit of love can only be approached alone."

By the time I found the station and got the right ticket and stood in the diesel haze at what I hoped was the right queue, I felt my energy draining away like water through a paper bag. How much longer? I hadn't brought a watch with me. I wasn't sure of the time. And I was getting hungry. The airplane food seemed to be absorbing energy rather than giving. How long would it take me to grab something to eat? What if the bus came while I was away from the line? It couldn't be much longer.

It was. A crowd of football fans spilled into the station. It seemed to me there might be too many of us for the bus, that I couldn't leave my spot in the line, even to take a pee, which I needed to do. I thought about leaving my little knapsack to hold my spot — but someone would probably walk off with it. It was dark when the bus pulled up and we were pushed inside by the press from behind. I was lucky to have a seat — the overflow stood in the aisles, singing and drinking and smoking and yelling with every bump and turn. I had no energy to fight my way back to the latrine. I probably could have pissed out the window and no one would have minded. If the window could have been opened.

Loud as it was, airless and foul, I couldn't keep my eyes open. My head bobbed, striking the window and rattling with the bus vibrations, then lurching to the other side and landing in the lap of an elderly woman who was sitting rigid and angry beside me. It was nearly midnight by the station clock when we pulled into St. Andrews. The passengers were subdued by then. The bus was quiet and dark, and wrapped in the stench of vomit. How happy to fight my way free of it, to breathe at last some cool, fresh air, to stand at the urinal and feel release.

I didn't have a place to stay. The first three inns I called were full, and I ran out of change for the phone. Nothing was open. Half an hour after I arrived, the train station closed behind me. So I wandered the streets in the October wind. I didn't know what to do. I hadn't really thought through what was supposed to happen once I got to St. Andrews. I had just assumed that I would find Mirele somehow — probably she would be walking on the street, in the campus — wherever the campus was. I would just have to keep my eyes open.

Which I did. Too cold to sit down, I walked the entire night, watched the black shop windows turn to silver and then to gold as the sun rose over the North Sea. This is not too much effort for love, I was thinking. I can do it. I can do it. This will make a good story. For my grandchildren.

Everything ached by nine-thirty when I walked into Mrs. Cane's Bed & Breakfast. Shivering, foggy-headed, I could barely sign in.

"Have you come from far?" Mrs Cane asked, raising her eyebrows.

"Yes," I nodded.

"And will you be needing some breakfast?"

She meant for the following morning, but my look must have convinced her that something right now would be appropriate.

"So what is it you're here for, lad?" Mrs. Cane asked later, as she came with my bacon and eggs and toast and sausage and orange juice and roast potatoes left over from the night before. "You've not come for our lovely weather?"

"You're not a golfer," she went on, "and I'd warrant you're a student, but term is already started, and you'd be in residence, not here."

She paused, waiting for me to fill in the details. I didn't say anything.

"Ay well, none of my business then, is it?" she said.

"I'm just . . . I'm going to visit a friend," I said.

"I knew it!" she said, her big hand slamming down on the table. "You're after a girl! I could see it right in your face, plain as day!"

I looked at her in amazement.

"So, come on love, tell me about it," she said, sitting down at the table, glowing with her accomplishment. There were three others in the tiny dining room; they all pressed towards me to hear.

"Don't be shy!" she said. "There's nothing more exciting than a young lad chasing after a girl!"

And so I told them, a little bit, and Mrs. Cane kept asking, and so I told them a little more.

"So where is she living then, this Mirele?" she asked. "That's an odd name, you know. But sometimes it's the most beautiful women who have the oddest names. Like David's niece, you know what they called her? Felicia. But she's got eyes would flip your feet out from under you. But anyway —"

"I don't know where she's living," I said.

"You don't have her address?"

"No. It wasn't on the card."

"But you have her phone."

"No."

"Ay, you're a brave one," she said, and the three other faces nodded.

It was Mrs. Cane who brought out the telephone directory and the phone so I could try the three M. Lewises and the two E. Lewises, in case she had gone by her formal name, Esmirelda. None of the guests left to do whatever business they had — I suppose I was too entertaining. After none of the Lewises was right, Mrs. Cane brought out the college directory. I phoned one M. Lewis who was Mary, and another who was Martin, and another who did not answer. The single E. was Evan Lewis who swore at me for waking him up.

"Well, she must be the one who was out," Mrs. Cane said. "Process of elimination. Just try her again a little later."

So I retreated to my room and watched the day grow greyer. I thought of my grandfather chasing after his Colleen in weather like this, their collars up, backs braced against the wind.

I called nine times. Mirele was not in.

In the afternoon the weather slackened to a steady mist, so I borrowed a raincoat that had belonged to the late Mr. Cane and wandered along part of the Old Course — there were a few hardy people playing — and the grey beach, and then into town. The rain picked up just as I happened upon a series of stone buildings that I took to be the university.

The playing fields were deep green and soggy and deserted, and the windows were opaque in the failing light.

I found a public phone booth and called. She wasn't in.

"Maybe she's gone away for the weekend," Mrs. Cane said, over dinner.

Maybe she had. I spent the Saturday and Sunday wandering the campus, trailing through the library, waiting in front of the residences, peering into passing faces. I wouldn't let myself call more than once an hour — it was getting expensive from a pay phone — and I would hang up after fifteen rings, whether she might be just coming in and running for the phone or not.

I started asking people. "Do you know a student named Mirele Lewis? She has black hair and very dark eyes and —"

"What's she studying?"

"I don't know."

"Hmmm . . . "

"She's about medium height and very thin and —"

I didn't call after midnight on Sunday. If she came in after that, I wasn't going to disturb her. I didn't want her to think that I was desperate.

The next morning I awoke before light and waited until after breakfast to try. "Hello, Mirele! Hi, yes, it's me!" I rehearsed in my head. "Yes, I got your card and I'm just doing a little travelling and I thought —"

The phone rang twenty-seven times before I put it down.

I tried once more in the morning and three times in the afternoon, and then just before dinner someone picked it up.

"Hello?" she said.

It was just one word, but her accent was so unique I knew immediately it was her. Thank God.

"Hi, it's me!" I said.

"Excuse me, who?"

"James! Listen, I got your card and I was just doing some —"

"James who?"

"Mirele?" Even as I said the name I knew it wasn't her voice after all.

"I'm very sorry. I seem to have gotten the wrong number. I'm terribly —"

"That's okay," she said, and then she went away.

I got out the college directory again and phoned the registrar's office. There was a long wait; I had to talk to several people, but they couldn't find Mirele registered anywhere. I pulled out Mirele's card. It was postmarked St. Andrews. She had written on it — "My programme is almost through — it's been grisly." It had seemed obvious to me that she was at the university. And yet, how clear now — and how muddy. "We went to Prestwick and watched the lights at the edge of the runway at night. It was like galaxies were speeding by." Where was Prestwick airport? I got out my tourist map. It was on the Firth of Clyde, on the wrong coast — nowhere near St. Andrews!

Was she at another university? Maybe she was at Oxford or Cambridge. Maybe I didn't have a clue in the world. I photocopied several pages of United Kingdom colleges and universities at the library, and I began calling them one by one — getting transferred, being put on hold, waiting through ring after ring for someone to pick up the phone. "Who? How do you spell that? What is her department?"

On and on, down the list, until I had spent £150 on the phone and still didn't know where Mirele was, if she was. I couldn't get over the feeling that she was right there, very close to me. How to find her? It occurred to me that I could phone the Canadian consulate in Jakarta, and talk to Mirele's father, and he would give me her address. I didn't know how much it would cost. My return ticket was paid for, but I still had to cover my room, and money was getting tight.

It's such an odd feeling to pick up a receiver and listen as the signal leaps from switch to switch, channel to channel, to ask for directory assistance half a planet away. It's so absurd! Carry my voice to Indonesia. Wake those people up. Have them be there at the end of the line when I can't even find a girl who might be living next door to me.

"Hello, Mr. Lewis, sir, this is James Kinnell, phoning from Scotland. Do you remember me?"

"Of course, yes!" the voice came back, a little foggy, as if he was still living a few blocks away but had had a bit too much to drink. "How are you? What are you doing in Scotland?"

"I'm fine, thank you sir. I'm happy to be able to get you. I'm just travelling for a bit and I was hoping you might have Mirele's address. I have this card from her —"

He didn't answer right away. I thought at first that the line might have been interrupted and so I began to repeat myself.

"No, it's all right," he said sharply, as if he was beside me now. "If you got a card from her recently then you're way ahead of us. We haven't heard from her in over two years."

He said several more things that I couldn't really process. Then he had me read him the card.

"She's getting married is she?" he said in a flat tone. "Well, that's news to us. Sorry I can't help you."

I was sorry too, and meant to say it, but the words didn't quite fall in line. Her father said, "We lost control of her really at this bloody school here. And then she disappeared and we had no idea where she'd gone until we learned she was with you and your mother. She stayed with us for a while after that but then she took off again. My wife is sick about it. We're both sick about it."

I asked him what had happened in the school in Jakarta and he said, "Well, you know, with the head master and everything. The affair. I almost took the man out and shot him myself. He lost his job at least. She must have talked about it."

No, she hadn't, but suddenly I didn't have the heart to hear. Before he let me go he made me promise to get in touch with him if I found her. I said that I would.

"Ay, then, you're leaving us?" Mrs. Cane said as I stood by her desk with my little pack, handing back the raincoat she had leant me. "It's a shame you not finding your Mirele."

"Yes," I said, looking at my shoes.

"The postmaster, Mr. Davies, might be able to help you, you know. She might not have a phone, you see. But she would have an address. He's a friend of mine."

"That's okay," I said.

"But it's a shame to come all this way and not find her," she said. "Mr. Davies normally wouldn't give out the information but he's a soft man inside, if you know what I mean. I mean, not to look at him. But he's a friend of mine, you see —"

"Thank you, no," I said, shaking my head. "I think I found what I needed to find." And then I kissed her on the cheek.

After paying my bill I didn't have enough for bus fare and so I set out to hitchhike back to Heathrow. The rain was falling in a steady, icy drizzle, the kind that wears you down from a strong young mountain to a moss-covered rock. My feet were cold and I was hungry and it was strange how my eyes still looked out for her, even as I was walking along the road with my thumb out. Maybe she would just be stepping out of a coffee shop and I would catch her eye and we would start to talk, and she would smile and there, the air would be clear, all those sad things from the past wouldn't matter any more.

When the first car stopped I almost didn't get in. Maybe if I waited a little bit longer . . . The driver was a middle-aged man in a thick coat with an accent so strong I almost couldn't understand him. He left me off in a little town on the coast and then a farmer drove me three and a half miles and then I waited four hours in the cold and dark for another car to stop. I started to shiver from deep inside, my feet shuffling involuntarily, my teeth clattering. Was this the bottom? Was this the very worst that I would feel for love? Would I survive this night and make it home to heal?

I wasn't entirely coherent when the next car finally stopped. I piled in beside the driver without really checking to see who it was. It was warm inside, out of the wind and rain — that was all that counted. I could barely keep my eyes open.

"So where are you going to?" the old man asked, and I told him. I don't remember what he replied. I don't think I even waited to hear how far he could bring me before I was asleep.

I woke up with a start sometime in the night. It occurred to me that I'd fallen asleep while driving; that I was waking up just in time to save myself but I couldn't find the steering wheel — it wasn't anywhere it was supposed to be. Then I looked over and there was the old man smiling at me.

"No from around here, are ye?" he said, and he passed over a small wineskin. "That'll warm you up," he said, and it did.

It's hard to explain what happened then. Nothing really changed, and yet in the next few moments it was as if the roof had slid off the car and all the stars in the night sky were suddenly revealed for what they were — and I can't even tell you what they were. I just had this glimpse of a certainty that nothing that happens in life is an accident — that we are on a journey that we take step by step and every step is new and every one is very old, and we only get to see that a few times in our lives.

"First I'll talk," the old man said as we sped on through the night. "Then you can talk, and I will talk again."

PART II

The Memory Holes of Garland Rose

NINE

I slip sometimes into what I think of as a memory hole — a daydream that is in fact a memory, events from long ago carved into me like slippery grooves down a hill. It usually comes on me when I'm sitting, very still, but sometimes in a client's office, as we're going over some more or less complicated renovation and I know either I won't do it or they won't want me to do it, and there's no point anymore except long streams of words must come out before the outcome is clear. We're all bright in some way, I know. Mine is that I seem to know where things are going long before other people do. Either that's it or the other people need to hear themselves talk for much longer than I do.

Daddy was like that. He desperately needed to explain things to me that I already understood, or else I understood that they wouldn't apply to me and yet he insisted on telling me. I think he was lonely that way. I think with me he had a captive audience and he knew it and there was no escape. My dream (which is actually a memory) is that it's winter and we're alone in the North Pole, which is to say the fourteenth hole, the furthest from any shelter — a farmer's field is adjacent and the woods are behind us a good drive and a three-wood and the wind is whipping the snow in our faces. I'm strapped in the toboggan, encased in a yellow snowsuit, wrapped in blankets, a fake-furry hood from the Salvation Army cutting off my vision without stopping the wind from freezing my cheeks.

He's ahead, pulling me with a rope tied to the toboggan, a big man who'll get smaller over the years. He's wearing a light jacket, a windbreaker, with three sweaters on under-neath, and a big pair of leather gloves and a toque with a bright red leaf on it, also from the Salvation Army. Some-times he crashes through a snowdrift and flounders to his waist, pulling me up the slope, then turning to watch as I slide down.

I clutch his six-iron, his never-fail club, his Excalibur. He uses it for chipping, for clever curving shots out of the woods, for impossible lies in the rough, and for snow. It's es-pecially good in the snow. He has tried other clubs — his four-wood, his pitching wedge, his three-iron — but nothing seems to work as well out of the snow as his six-iron. He has told me this hundreds of times, and is telling me again, his voice turning whiny in the wind like a weak radio signal.

"Whatever happens, you need to have an escape club. Something you can improvise with. You can imagine the shape of the shot just as you look at the lie, and that feeling travels down your fingers right into the club."

He gives me these pointers as if he is the teacher and I will be tested on them someday, but in fact they are for him-self. I'm here mostly as a sounding board. He doesn't expect me to get up and swing the club. Sometimes I say something and he looks back at me as if he has forgotten I'm here. The six-iron drags in the snow as I'm pulled along, and I watch the trail it makes behind me, feel the bounce of the club in my fingers, press harder to make sure it doesn't slip out. Once I dropped it and yelled and yelled and it was hardly even windy but Daddy didn't hear me, he was talking to himself, motioning with his hands, working out something in his mind. So we went for fifty yards before I finally got his attention, and then he turned back and ran for his club in a way he has never run for me when I've fallen down or am upset. He's always calm and detached then. But with the six-iron temporarily lost it was as if bombs were falling and he had to get to the shelter.

(We're learning about bombs in school and practise evacuating when the alarm goes off. You have to shut the heavy drapes and close your eyes immediately if there's a big flash and be careful because the glass might blow in like that, *whoosh!* Miss Reynolds has her hair long and straight down her back and sometimes wears pants to class and plays her guitar most days, and we sing *Where Have all the Flowers Gone?* and she doesn't wear a bra. She bounces which makes the boys giggle and on cold days her nipples stick out when she wears a turtleneck. Stephanie Briggs has had her ears pierced already and another girl, Susan, who's almost as tall as Miss Reynolds, one day wore pantyhose instead of tights, she showed us in the bathroom. She said her mother had been too busy to notice.)

These things — pantyhose, pierced ears, nipples — don't apply to my father. They are beyond what he understands and so I don't discuss them with him. He doesn't do well about new subjects. He can tell you all about backswings, about balance and lateral shifts and whipping your hands through upon impact. He knows about steel shafts, forged heads, persimmon drivers. He knows sixty-two different putting stances. None of it applies to me, and nothing of what's important to my life applies to him, except that I'm strapped to the toboggan. He insists that I'm big enough now to ski and that I could keep up with him, and I insist that I'm big enough now that he can leave me alone when he goes out, so it's a stand-off. He won't leave me, I won't ski. So I'm strapped, and as I'm pulled along I think of the wind freezing my feet, then my calves and knees, and how I won't say anything, I'll be the brave little stupid obedient girl who nearly dies but doesn't call out and then when Daddy sees it'll be too late, my legs will have to be amputated. I'll have to stay in bed and paint and in my spare time I'll invent the water-powered car that will save the world from pollution.

We get to the ball, white against the white snow. I never know how he finds it, but somehow it never seems to land in a deep spot and he always seems to know where to go. He takes the six-iron from me, sets up, waggles, and swings. The ball disappears immediately.

"Did you see it?"

"No," I say. I never see it.

"Just over there. Do you see? It rolled onto the pond."

He points to a blizzard of white.

"Daddy, I'm cold."

"It's right down on top of the pond," he says. "Should I take a stroke for that or not? What do you think?"

"Daddy, I'm freezing cold!"

"If this was summer, of course, I'd have to take a stroke. I'd never be able to play out of the pond. Not out of the middle like that, anyway. Out of the shallows the tricky part is taking into account the refraction of the light in the water. If you hit down where you think the ball is going to be you'll miss it —"

"Daddy, can we go home now?"

"Almost, honey. Two more holes to go. I'm three over in a snowstorm. Not bad, eh?"

On we pull, the six-iron dragging behind me, down the hill this time. It happens in my memory-hole the same way it happened for real.

"Daddy, that sign says *Danger — Deep Pond!*" I say when we are at the edge.

"What? Oh that. Don't worry about that. That's for the summer, that sign. Here, give me the club."

"But what if you fall through?"

"Oh for God's sakes, it's thirty below zero. Unless this is a spring-fed pond, it'll hold an elephant. It's amazing the ball would stop right in the middle like that, though, isn't it?"

"Daddy!"

"Don't over-react!" The ice at the shore crunches under his foot and he leaps onto the thick part, the stable part, looking back and grinning.

"When you're older," he says, twirling the club in his thick gloves as he walks, "don't be a carping woman. It'd break her heart if your mother found out you were growing up to be a carping woman. It shows such a profound lack of confidence —" and just as he pronounces the word there is a *bang* like a gunshot.

"Don't over-react!" he says, laughing, twirling the club. "It's just the ice adjusting itself. I can see down a couple of feet here. It's really clear. Why don't you come and have a look?"

I stay in the toboggan, freezing, shaking my head.

"You have to have confidence and courage," he says, coming up to the ball now, but yelling back at me as if I should be taking notes. "A life without confidence and courage . . . is not worth living. Now your mother," he says, lining up his feet, checking his grip, "was blessed with both. She didn't have any luck, mind you . . . but she had great courage and great confidence."

My mother is a black and white woman in a silver picture frame who's thinking about something as she looks down and pulls dark curls from her forehead. She wears a flower print dress and has beautiful cheekbones and the tendons on one side of her neck stick out as she turns, and a spot near her ear is very bright, as if the sun was trying to catch her eye but missed. She doesn't wear earrings, and I'll never meet her and never remember her except through this picture and Daddy's words. It's only when I'm older that it occurs to me to ask. "What makes you say she had great courage? What did she do — go out and fight bears?"

"No, she married me!" is the only answer I will get.

I watch the swing carefully, squint my eyes against the wind to see. There's the flash of the steel shaft and for the first time I see the ball take off, am able to keep track as it rises above the bleak white of the terrain and flies into the greyish white of the sky like a slow-motion bullet. It's so majestic I forget to breathe, the flight so perfect. So this is why boys throw stones. The ball heads down and I almost lose it when the snow white of the ground rises up again but no, there it is, a tiny grey spot on the hardened white dish where the green is lying frozen underneath.

"I saw it!" I yell and look back at Daddy, but he has disappeared, and where he was there's nothing but a black hole in the ice. There's no shout. The wind has suddenly stopped.

Then his head breaks the surface like a whale, water sputtering, the six-iron flashing in the air, an arc of droplets spraying all the way back to the shore where I'm strapped and bundled.

"Daddy! Daddy! Daddy!" I yell, fighting against the rope that's holding me in. He has tied it using a bowline, which he has tried over and over to get me to memorize, but I never did. He flounders in the ice, tries to pull himself up but the edge breaks and his head ducks under again. I scream again and pull at the knot and his head comes up again but he says nothing, only, "It's okay, Garland, I'm fine. Don't over-react, I'm fine."

But I am not. I pull and pull but the rope is frozen, and my Daddy is disappearing like the lovely lady in the silver frame I never met, going without a scream, without a word, except, "I'm fine. Don't over-react. I'm okay."

Then the chain support on the toboggan breaks and I'm up and running onto the ice. "Don't come out, honey! Garland! *I order you to go back!*" I keep going. "Don't take another step! I'm almost out! *Go back!*" I reach the edge where the black water is eating up the ice which is not a couple of feet, it's a couple of inches perhaps, and getting thinner all the time. "Give me the six-iron, Daddy. I'll pull you!" "You aren't strong enough! Get out of the way! *Garland!* But he has reached his six-iron to me anyway and I grab with my mittens and pull. I'm not strong enough, it's true, but I broke the chain on the toboggan, and maybe it doesn't take very much anyway, he just needs help to shift his balance. He inches his way out, not pulling too much on the six-iron, just a little. "Back up!" he says and I do, pulling and crying and pulling some more.

The ice breaks and breaks and breaks at the edge, then it holds, and he pulls himself out, so slowly, and I wonder will he freeze before he makes it, become a sculpture like in the Silver Fair? But it's all right. We crawl to the shore and he says, "This is all part of the programme," slapping himself as his pants and his jacket and his boots turn to ice. "Great for the legs, the adrenaline. Now don't drop that club or I'll be very angry, do you hear?" And so I don't, even as he picks me up and slings me over his shoulder.

"It gets the heart rate up," he says as we bump along, the snow stinging my face. "Good . . . for the shoulders . . . the arms . . . the lungs." He puffs for a few strides and the six-iron clumps against his ankle but he doesn't feel it. "It's exactly what I'm . . . missing . . . from my training. Grace under pressure. You can't know . . . if . . . you have it or not till . . . it's tested. Do you agree little girl?"

"Yes, Daddy!" I yell, my head bouncing against his back.

"I think . . . I think I need a song. Can you think of a song?"

There is only one song we ever sing, *Row row row your boat*, but I can't find my voice now. He doesn't wait for me. *Row row row your boat, gently down the stream*, his voice too relaxed, as if he's acting the part. *Merrily, merrily, merrily, merrily . . . life is but a dream!* Bump and lurch we go and then he falls right into the snowdrift.

"Daddy! Get up! Come on!" I say, hitting his shoulder. "Come on! *Row row row your boat!*" I yell, right into his ear. "Keep singing!"

"Just kidding," he says, in a little, weird voice as he lurches to his feet. "Where were we?" and he reaches to pick me up.

"Don't carry me! Just run on your own. I'm okay!"

He looks up strangely.

"*Go!*" I yell in his ear, and he responds, dumbly, picking up his feet and moving forward.

He says I shouldn't be a carping woman but there is no other way to get him to keep moving. I have to yell at him because he just wants to lie down in the snowbank. So I yell, "*Keep going! Keep going! This is all in the programme!*" I hit him sometimes with the six-iron — whack! on his bum, whack! on his thighs — to keep him moving. It's horrible but I can't think of anything else. He doesn't seem to know what's happening. I drive him all the way up the ninth fairway, right to the deserted parking lot where we've left the car, and I yell at him when all he wants to do is lean against the outside.

"Get in! Get in! Turn on the heater!"

But he doesn't seem to hear me anymore so I open the door and push him till he folds himself into the passenger seat.

"Where are the keys? Daddy, look in your pocket — where are the keys?"

He closes his eyes now, his head nodding forward. Frost has turned his eyelashes white. His face is ghostly blue.

"*Don't fall asleep! Get the keys!*" I yell, loud enough right into his ear to make him jump, his head knocking against the window.

"They're in my pocket," he says, very calmly, like he's telling me where the butter is. "My hands aren't working. You'll have to get them."

I beat his frozen pocket with my mitt till my hand will go in, then free the keys and jangle them in front of his face.

"Which is the right one?"

"You can't drive little girl," he says, but he nods at the big one with the square sides.

"It's all in the programme," I tell him.

I've never been allowed to start the car, but there are lots of things I know before other people anyway, and who else is there? It's hard to see over the dashboard, but if I sit up I can get my foot on the pedals. The big one is the brake, obviously. The tall one the accelerator. R must mean reverse, but where is F for forward? I try N, but nothing, then D and whoops! There we go!

Not very quickly. It isn't far to our house anyway. When we get there Daddy is awake a little and walks in all by himself, but I can't get his clothes off, they're frozen on. So he lies down in the living room and I pile on blankets, then call the ambulance and wait for it to come.

TEN

When I first see him I know he'll ask me out if he gets half the chance. His eyes give him away. I've been taking the meditation classes for almost six months, usually going Tuesdays at seven, but had to miss one because of work and so tonight I drop by the Thursday class. There are more people than I expect and at first I'm not sure there will be a mat for me. The instructor is Alex's husband, who doesn't have Alex's way in the world. When Alex walks in a room the lights seem to brighten. She looks directly in your eyes and there is always a smile in her manner. She's no slave to her appearance, but she's beautiful. She doesn't flop around in a gymnasium, but she's healthy. She doesn't work very hard at conversation, but delightful things come out. Alex's husband seems much more ordinary: there's a pallor to his skin, circles under his eyes, a pudginess and lack of fire. And though he says the same sorts of words about meditation that Alex does, it's as if he has just read them the day before. When they come from Alex , they seem to be direct from her inner magma.

(Whatever "inner magma" is — it's the sort of term that is evocative of the primordial fires within when Alex uses it, and sounds like New Age puffery when her husband tries.)

I don't listen to Alex's husband after the first few minutes, but it's hard to ignore the young man in the corner. He's very tall and reedy and athletic-looking, and he has trouble crossing his legs comfortably. And he just keeps staring at me.

After a while I'm able to ignore him and Alex's husband

and sink into my own thoughts. I'm not supposed to do that in meditation, I know — I'm supposed to concentrate on my breathing, and when a thought comes I should mentally say "thought" and have it go away. I should "ground" myself, feel my seat in the world as it is, large and profound. (The world, that is, not my seat.) I've tried all that, but what I really like is having the chance to slip into a memory hole. I know it's all thoughts, and they have nothing to do with my seat in the world as it is, large and profound . . . but it's so easy to close my eyes and there I am sitting on that bench in the hallway in the hospital, with my boots on and my snowsuit zipped up and my mitts still on my hands. The bright lights hurt my eyes and the hospital air hurts my lungs. A man in green sits beside me too close and says, "You were tobogganing and your father fell through the ice, is that how it happened?"

"No," I say, boiling inside my clothes, but too scared to take them off.

"Well, maybe you can tell me what happened, then."

"He was golfing," I say, "and I told him not to go on the ice but he wouldn't listen. He never listens."

"Golfing?"

I nod.

"In a snowstorm?"

"It's in the programme," I say.

"What programme?"

"My father's training programme. He's going to be a professional golfer. He's going to be better than Jack Nicklaus. It's in the training."

The man looks at me like everyone else does when we explain it to them, and so I say, "He was three over par in a snowstorm. Not bad, eh?"

(I shift my position and look up for a moment. He's still

looking at me, the young man, like he can read my thoughts but can't understand them.)

It's much later. My snowsuit is off. I'm not wearing my boots anymore but have stepped in a small puddle of melting ice on the floor and the feet of my blue tights are soaked. They let me go in to see Daddy. It's late in the afternoon and the light from the window makes everything look like a black and white photograph. Daddy is sitting up in bed, looking out the window at the snow driving sideways across the glass. He turns to look at me. His hands are bandaged.

"Must have been a spring-fed pond," he says. "They never freeze properly." And he laughs, like it is a great thing to know.

He says, "Ben Hogan came back from a car accident to win the U.S. Open three times," and I don't say anything, his face looks so white. "He wasn't supposed to walk again. He was finished. There was no hope. But after his accident he played his best major tournament golf in his whole career. He won the Masters twice, the British Open the very first time he played it." His eyes gleam. He says, "I'll have to adjust my grip. I was thinking about doing it anyway. The trick is to not over-compensate with the right hand. Then what would happen? Can you tell me that?"

"You'd hook the ball," I say in a little voice.

"Exactly! That's right. Exactly Hogan's problem, when he was younger. When the pressure was on him, he'd snap-hook it into the woods."

The colour comes back to his face when he talks about Hogan.

"Daddy — are you all right? Are you going to die?"

"Yes," he says solemnly, and I take a step back and find it hard to breathe. "We're all going to die. It's the one thing you can say with certainty. We're all going to die. Not even taxes are for certain — some people wriggle out of taxes pretty well. But death will come for us all. And then do you know where we'll be?"

"With Mommy," I say, my voice still little.

"Yes, exactly," he says. "And with the two fingers I just lost on my left hand."

"Come out of the meditation slowly," says Alex's husband, his voice sort of fish-lipped, like he's talking in a diving suit under the ocean. "Slowly regain awareness of your body, your temporal space, the channels of your everyday thoughts . . . " The tall young man tries to stand and his joints crack like rifle shots. He looks like he's still in university. Probably his eyes aren't very good. As soon as he gets close to me he'll realize how old I am.

"There's tea as usual in the den," Alex's husband says and I stretch my legs, and look around without catching anyone's eye. This is not my usual group. I don't know anyone here. I won't stay.

But the tall young man is at the doorway. He's wearing loose dark pants and a white cotton shirt without a collar, slightly wrinkled, and his feet are bare still. They are long and wide and his toes are hairy — very male feet. I duck under his gaze as I collect my coat. He says, "I'm not sure I've noticed you in this class before."

It's a bold thing for a young man to say and it puts me off-balance. His eyes are very intensely blue. They're unmarried eyes if I've ever seen them.

"No, I usually go to the Tuesday class," I say, and then, after a pause, "it's a little smaller."

We could introduce ourselves. We could talk about who we are and what we do and why we meditate, but nothing is said. His arm is slightly blocking the doorway. He's so tall I could easily duck under, but I hesitate — the motion would make me feel like a child.

There are a lot of strange people who meditate. I suppose that could include me, but I don't think of myself as strange. Actually, I think of myself as one of the normal ones. I almost say, "You know, I don't really meditate when I come here. This is just my way of being with a bunch of people and staying quiet." But of course I don't say that. He's a complete stranger. I'm not sure he'd understand. He'd think me one of the weirdos too. He might laugh and think I was joking, or not laugh and think I was being serious.

So I duck under his arm and say, "Good night," and feel his eyes on my back as I leave.

ELEVEN

"Daddy. What have you done to the basement!"

I'm home from camp exhausted after three weeks of pine needles up my bathing suit, of waking up in the middle of the night screaming at snakes, and floundering around pretending to swim; of dumping the canoe just by stepping in it, hiking through the woods in the rain singing just because somebody ordered us to and hearing about Liza who's had her period already; of eating fried eggs and oatmeal every morning, thinking at night in my lumpy bunk, "I've now finished Day Five; there are only Sixteen More Days to Go"; of wondering why am I the only one in Raccoons who doesn't have breasts and when Laurel the head counsellor says, "Has anyone here ever tried to play golf?" shaking my head along with everyone else, No, I haven't a clue.

"*Daddy! What have you done?*"

"Like it?" he says, going ahead of me down the stairs, clumping with his right foot now because of the toes he lost. "It's an exact replica of the ninth green at Augusta. Well, a little smaller I guess, and you have to ignore the support poles. You have no idea how hard it was to get it this smooth."

The basement is full of swales and hollows, with sunken golf holes here and there, swooping concrete covered by felt so green it hurts the eyes.

"What happened to the furniture?" The basement used to be full of furniture from Mother's family in Austria, huge sideboards and dressers and dining room tables with matching chairs, and lamps and bedboards, too large for any of our rooms. It was all supposed to go to me when I grew up and moved away. It's the story Daddy always told me.

"Don't worry about it," he says, walking out onto the felt, picking up the putter leaning against the stairs and taking a ball out of his pocket. "You should have seen the dust in here when I was sanding down the concrete. It was a good thing you were away — your allergies would have gone crazy."

"But where's my furniture?" I cry.

"I didn't realize there are actual industrial sanders for smoothing down concrete," he says. "Of course, you couldn't really get it down as smooth as you need. I tried my hardest, and then — *brainstorm!* — I laid down a quarter-inch covering of foam, and then the felt on top of that. Watch your shoes, honey — this is like a big pool table. You don't want to rip the covering."

"But Daddy!" I say, sitting on the bottom stair. "That was supposed to be my furniture for when I'm grown up! Where did you put it? Is somebody looking after it?"

"I'll tell you what happened," he says, lining himself up and then stroking a putt up the swale and around. It lips out on one of the holes then continues down the hill, right to the bottom against the wall, twenty feet away. "You see that, that's just like at Augusta!" he says. "You get above the hole on number nine and forget it. All you have to do is get the ball rolling and you're off the green. Automatic bogey."

He walks down the swale to get his ball and then putts it back up, ten feet short.

"You see that? That's realistic too — almost everybody leaves it short trying to go up that hill. Because it's so fast coming down, it's deceptive. I really had to be careful what felt I chose."

"Did you sell my furniture, Daddy?"

"Well," he says, putting it in finally. "It was the only solution. We had a flood in here while you were away. I have no idea what happened to the washing machine — it just went berserk. I was out, and when I came back — well, there was about a foot of water in here and the tide was rising. Most of the stuff looked ruined to me. So I called a friend of mine who's a dealer, just to have him come and have a look, you know. Most of that stuff was so old, a bit of water and it was ready to just rot away. Anyway, he came up with what I thought was an acceptable offer. It was only when the stuff was completely cleared away, and I saw the potential for this space — well, work had to be done on it anyway, it was so wet down here. I just got this brainstorm. I figure we've added ten thousand dollars to the value of the house. If the buyer's a golfer at all."

"So how was camp?" he says, finally.

On Tuesday, work is going badly and I very nearly miss the meditation session again. A couple argues for forty-five minutes over what to do with the upstairs of a gabled Victorian town home they aren't even sure they're going to buy. The man wants to clear everything out, put in skylights and a waterbed and, in the very middle, surrounded by no walls, an enormous jacuzzi. ("But what kind of extra support beams are we talking about here? That's all I'm asking. I'm just exploring options," he says over and over.) The woman wants three separate rooms, a cosy little bedroom with a feather bed and south-facing windows, a sewing room adjacent, and another room on the other side just for sitting still and reading or writing letters. They go back and forth, the man's temple of love and the woman's re-creation of a doll's house.

I cut them off at twenty to seven, leave my diagrams and a few photos from samples, and ask them to get in touch with me when they've decided so I can put together my proposal. But that's not good enough — they want me to draw up plans for both visions.

"Fine," I say, nodding. Maybe they have lots of money. I rush home, throw on my sweatsuit and bolt out again, supperless. I don't want to have to go again on Thursday night, and I don't want to miss my session for a whole week. It's either this or therapy. I'm late again, and flustered when I arrive. I make too much noise fighting the front door. My shoes won't come off without a struggle. The group is already sitting when I blunder in. Still, only two people open their eyes at my commotion: Alex, and the young man from last Thursday.

It surprises me to see him. My heart starts to pump. He's wearing blue jeans ripped in one knee and a white t-shirt that says, "Save the Temagami Forests." He's long and thin and his skin is too tanned. He hasn't shaved today and his hair loops around his ears in black curls.

Alex doesn't say a word, but I know at once it's all right to pull up a mat and settle in. The closest one open is right beside the young man. I take the one on the opposite side of the room, near the door.

It takes the longest time for my heart to stop pounding, but I fall eventually into another memory hole, in the autumn when I've started high school and I'm hurrying home. My new text books are heavy and the air is cold and I'm seized with this certainty that my life will always be like this: that I'll always be in school and it'll always be just the start and there will be years to go before I'll be grown up and won't have to carry books. I'm hurrying home because I have to get dinner ready for Daddy who's just started a new job at the car plant. He's now a foreman which means he must work much longer hours, but he's not earning any more money. No, he has worked out a plan so that he'll be able to retire earlier with his full pension. Then, of course, he'll devote himself entirely to his life's passion. If there's anything left of him.

He'll be completely free the year I graduate from high school. That is when I'll go off somewhere to university and his pension will kick in and life will begin. He's going to sell the house then and drive around the continent playing tournament golf. He already has a big road atlas and knows the names of the towns on the PGA tour which he'll visit one after the other, playing Monday to Wednesday to qualify, and then if he does well, Thursday and Friday to get in the money, and if he's still alive — it's his word, "alive" — Saturday and Sunday to try to win.

Sunday night he'll drive like the devil to make it to the next event.

If he does really well he'll get his tour card and won't have to qualify week after week. Or he could get his card at the tour qualifying school, but he's prepared for failure there. He'll learn top-level tournament golf at his own pace, and it'll be more glorious, more Hoganlike — to rise from the lowly qualifiers, at age fifty-two, with a physical handicap, to beat the young men through discipline and hard work and desire.

This is the plan taking shape ever since my mother was killed. He never tells me how she died. I find out years later when I'm finally in university and doing a research project which involves looking at microfilm newspapers. January 17, 1957, whizzes past me, the day of my birth. And the notice eight days later: "Born to Irv and Monika Carlson, Garland Rose, six pounds, three ounces. Good poise for a rookie." Daddy put in the announcement. My mother was supposedly furious with him for a week over the last line. (It's easy to zip forward a week in microfilm. It blurs past you, the printing presses clacking and surging, the new edition spinning till it stops, the headline loud as the machines.)

NEW MOTHER KILLED IN BUS ACCIDENT!
Inquiry to be held

There she is on the front page, the same picture of my mother as has hung in silver all those years in our home, with her eyes looking down and her curls falling away and that spot of overexposure, even in the newspaper photo. Daddy always says it's the only photo of her he has. No wedding photos? What about when she came home from the hospital with me? There are pictures of me as a newborn, but always alone in the bassinet. No arms are there to hold me.

The newspaper article doesn't say much about her or her

death. She had been stepping off the side door of a bus and turned to say something to someone inside and the doors had closed, catching her scarf. She was able to run for a bit but then slipped and fell beneath the wheels. People screamed at the driver but he was deaf in one ear. He had been too close to a bomb in the Korean War. Mother was dead in a few seconds. Everything was blamed on the new type of bus they were trying out, because the mirrors left large blind spots and the bus was too long. Besides being unsafe, it also tended to get stuck in the snow.

That's the last line in the story: nothing at all about my mother beyond the fact that she had just given birth. The focus is on the bus, the fact that besides all its other faults, it tended to get stuck in the snow.

So in my memory hole I'm sitting by the microfilm machine in the university library, my notes open on my lap, the page from 1957, slightly crooked, blurred on three edges, staring back at me: the record cold snap, students protesting in the Ukraine, the puppet government in Hungary. "In This Issue," says the little box in the one corner not blurry: "Do Most Women Worry About Their Figures? Yes . . . page 7." And right beside it the story about my mother. I sit there weeping for over an hour, till closing time. The lights flicker overhead and so I know it's time to go. I turn off the machine, rewind the tape, fiddle it into the box and onto the returns shelf, and then I walk into the cold night air.

The feeling envelopes me again as I sit, like there's a mudslide in my mind and a bank that used to be firm has now collapsed into the river no longer water but not earth either, rather a soup of the two. Everyone around me is concentrating on their breathing and thinking no thoughts and finding their seat in the world, and I'm crying silent, cleansing tears, seeping down my cheeks, salt on my lips, dripping onto my clothes.

When Alex starts to bring us out of the meditation I get up quietly and leave, picking up my shoes instead of putting them on, slinging my jacket over my shoulder, walking out barefoot. Once more the young man's eyes are on my back as I leave.

TWELVE

I come upon him by accident some days later in the super market. I don't recognize him at first — he's dressed in a tweed jacket and corduroy pants, a shirt and tie and leather walking shoes, nicely polished. He's even taller than I remembered him, pushing the cart slowly down the aisle, pausing to look at breakfast cereals. Sitting in his cart is a little girl, perhaps three.

I stay behind, don't let him see me. At the cat food section I look over the thirty-seven varieties, thankful that I don't own a cat. He moves on. I follow them. He has an easy way with the child, stopping to joke with her, to point something out, then moving her past some eye-level candy she wants.

They go to the meat section, I head for the vegetables. It's disturbing to think that just seeing someone I don't even know can make the floor feel so gritty under my shoes, the lights brighter. I have no heart for picking through broccoli.

I'm sure he didn't see me. I hoist a five pound bag of potatoes in my cart and even as I'm doing it I think — I rarely eat
potatoes. But I can't be bothered to take the bag out of my
cart. I can't think of what else I wanted to get and head off to
the checkout, overflowing with after-work shoppers just like
me, hungry, tired, irritable. The shortest line naturally takes
the longest — a man argues over the price of tahina and a
woman with only four items decides to cash a cheque and
spends five minutes looking through her purse for identifi-
cation. I wait, shifting from foot to foot. I want to get out of
these clothes. I want to get home. I don't want him to see me
here.

Just as the checkout girl clears the cheque I turn to pull
my cart through and there he is, staring at me as if he has
made quite a discovery. "Who's that lady?" the little girl says
and I turn my eyes away instinctively, reasoning that it's still
not too late to pretend I don't know him, because after all I
don't know him, we've not been introduced.

The girl checks me through and I fumble through my
purse for the money. A feeling of weirdness touches everything — my face is burning and my hands are cold. I have
this sudden thought that my hair must look a mess — I've
left it too long and he must see that. Then I'm through and
walking very quickly. I have trouble with the automatic, fool-
proof, confounded door which now won't open, not if I stand
here, not if I push or pull, or curse it. I go over to the IN
door and get tangled with a woman struggling to herd four
children in. She says, "Tim, will you step aside and let the
lady through?" and Tim says, "But she's going out the IN
door!" and then he says to me, "You're *weird*, lady!"

"I'm sorry, the other door is broken," I say and the woman
says, "Timmy, you apologize right now, that was such a rude
thing to say!" and by the time I have apologized again, and

the woman has apologized, and Timmy, unrepentant, has weaseled his way inside, they are behind me again, the young man with his daughter.

I make it half-way into the parking lot without turning my head or saying a word, and then my bag breaks, the sack of potatoes landing on the eggs and four apples spilling out and rolling away. When I kneel down my pantyhose runs halfway up my leg.

"Look at *that* — there's egg *everywhere!*" the little girl says with glee. The young man is carrying her with his left arm and three bags of groceries in his right. He puts down all his bundles and stoops to help me. "I'm all right," I say, putting what I can back into the torn bag, leaving the eggs to rot on the pavement.

"Can I help you carry it?" he asks, straightening up.

"Oh, yes, sure," I say. "You hardly have anything to carry yourself."

"That's okay," he says, "Cedes can walk, can't you honey?"

"No!" she says, crawling up his leg and pulling at his arm. He picks up the sack of potatoes and asks, "Where's your car?"

I point to the silver Volvo in the corner and we walk towards it, the young man carrying all his groceries and most of mine with his girl holding onto his trouser-leg and fussing the whole way.

"Why are we going over here?"

"Because this is where the woman's car is."

"But why do we have to go over here?" she repeats.

"Cedes — you just be quiet for awhile, will you honey?"

"*I don't want to go over here! Why do we have to go over here?*"

"Now see here, young lady . . ." he starts to say.

"It's okay, it's fine, I'm fine now," I say, reaching for my groceries.

"Cedes, we're trying to help this woman," he says. We are

stopped now in the middle of a lane and the little girl twists her whole body in the effort to not go along. "We're just trying to do something nice . . . "

She shakes her head vigorously.

"Listen," I say, "It's okay. I have this effect on children, you can tell."

But he doesn't listen to me. "Stop pulling at my hand," he says to the girl.

I manage to rescue my groceries. "Thanks very much anyway," I say, walking away. "I'm sure she'll feel better as soon as I go."

"Cedes —"

I give her a little wave.

"Her mother really has done a poor job of instilling some manners —"

Yes, sure, blame it on your wife.

"I'll see you on Tuesday," he says, picking up the little girl who is now in tears.

It's such a casual remark I forget to say, "I beg your pardon?" or "I'm sorry, have we met?"

He walks away with Cedes in one arm and groceries in the other, a purposeful stride, as if he can handle any challenge in life, just pick it up and go, the heavier the better. But what does he want with me? I wonder, fiddling with my keys and watching him walk away. He turns to look back. What does he want with me?

THIRTEEN

"Intuition is the most important instinct in life," Daddy says. We're driving in the dark on a back road, the gravel passing beneath us, the sounds muffled by the Great Big Car Daddy drives. Moonlight shines over my shoulder, and Daddy turns off the headlights to steer by "feel," touching the wheel now when he feels the shoulder on his left, on his right, on his left again. It's not dark outside really but silver, the fenceposts of the farm fields giving off a dull glow in the October air. Daddy flicks on the lights again as we enter a patch of fog, and it's as if we're in a silver tunnel, are miners with those lights on their helmets. It's better in the dark.

"Intuition is the oldest, most primitive, most experienced part of your brain," he says. "The one that knows first, automatically, and you don't even know how it knows. By smell first maybe. Who knows what we can smell and we don't even know we're smelling it? You get the rest of the brain involved and it's like levels of bureaucracy getting in on the decision. The Department of Common Sense writes up a memo. The Intellectual Input Agency agrees to bring the matter before a Standing Committee on Interdepartmental Affairs and prepares a brief. Finance and Administration demands to be heard. Before you know it a simple matter has become very cloudy. There's no heart left. The original, dead-accurate certainty is lost beneath an office-floor of files and considerations."

His voice is flat and low in the car. The humour doesn't come out at all. You have to be able to see his eyes for that. We roll through the fog. I've not been following where we're going and yet I know already. I'm not surprised when we take the turn. I know already the climb of the hill and the sound of the parking lot. He doesn't have to tell me about intuition.

"It's the one thing that gets lost most among players today," he says as we get out of the car, the clunk of the closing doors swallowed by the empty space around us. "Everyone is going by a system now, and I blame Nicklaus for it. He's the slowest, most robotic player ever. He knows the exact distance to the hole of every tree stump, sand trap and garbage can on the golf course. For every single shot you can see him going through his routine like some pilot getting ready for take-off. Propeller? Check! Flaps? Check! Radio? Check! Altimeter? Check! On and on and on, down the list. Thinking every muscle through its movement before he swings. Watch him as he stands over a putt. God! Thirty seconds, a minute, a minute and a half, rock still, *thinking* the ball into the hole. No wonder he's so intimidating. Everyone goes around trying to imitate him. But what nobody realizes — what Nicklaus himself probably doesn't realize — is that the strength of his game is his ability to come up with a great, inventive, courageous shot in a moment of crisis. Like that one-iron on seventeen at Pebble Beach — through the gales, laughing at the ocean, *rap!* right off the centre of the flag. At the exact moment he needed it. That kind of shot has nothing to do with checking the altimeter. It has everything to do with courage, which is married to intuition, the full partner of intuition. He could feel it in his hands, in his feet, in the way the club came back. He could smell it in the grass and the salt air and the rub of paint off the tee when he hit the shot."

He has his clubs out of the trunk now and we walk in the darkness towards the first tee. There's no wind at all and the night air is silent and feels like chilled hands on your throat.

Nothing he does surprises me anymore. He's going to play golf in the dark, and he lectures me about Nicklaus, who's the opposite of Hogan, hydraulics and robotics against fire and steel. There's the smell of coming winter and the tip of my nose is cold.

"How will you see the ball?" I ask as he tees it up on the first tee. Of course all this doesn't apply to me; I don't think it any more, I just know it. I'm not even here to carry his clubs. I'm just supposed to walk with him and listen and ask questions.

"I won't," he says. "I'll feel it on the moment of impact. You can know exactly where it's going by that fraction of a second on the clubface." He brings out his driver and swooshes the air twice, warming up. He has developed a new grip — double-fisted almost, fingers of both hands interlaced, almost on top of one another. He says losing two fingers has helped him. Otherwise he never would have thought of developing this new grip which gives him better control over the torque, whatever that means.

I can process the words but they don't apply to me.

He says, "There should be only one, at most two things you think about when you make your swing. It won't be the same thing for every game, though. That's where the robots make their mistake — thinking this thing can be broken down, mechanized, made absolute. A swing is organic. It's constantly growing or shrinking, living or dying, breathing, changing . . . like making love." On this last comment he looks over at me to see if he has embarrassed me. "It needs constant appraisal, nurturing, maintenance. But it'll be different things that need attending to at different times. Tonight, for me, it's lateral shift. I've been getting away from it. Instead of shifting my weight back and then forward, I've been staying in the middle and simply pivoting. Mechanically elegant, but I'm losing power. I get twenty more yards on my drive if I remember my lateral shift. But last week it was something different. It was my grip. I was relaxing, actually adjusting my fingers in the middle of the swing. If I hit the ball perfectly, great! But if I'm the slightest bit off then the club twists in my hands. Too firm, though, and the fluidity is cut right off. Slice the ball into the next field. Do you see what I mean? It's a series of constant adjustments."

He swings and hits the ball into the black, pauses, listening.

"Sand trap," he says, finally. He picks up his bag and we start walking.

It's not my job to run ahead and find the ball. He doesn't tee up a ball and insist I try to hit it. I don't want to hit it anyway. I don't even want to be here. But he doesn't know that. He has no idea that all his precious lectures don't apply to me in any way whatsoever.

When we get to the sandtrap there's no ball. The sand is just a smudge of silver in the black. It's possible that if there's a ball here we wouldn't even see it. But Daddy walks around and around the bunker, convinced the ball must be there. "I could feel the fade as it came off the club," he says, "and I was sure it sounded like sand when it hit. Didn't you think so?"

"I didn't hear it," I say, standing with my arms crossed, looking at him, not the ground where the ball might be. It's cold. I'm going to start shivering soon. Whatever we do, that always seems to be part of the programme.

He searches the turf around the sandtrap, by the big tree that dominates the right-hand side of the fairway, then into the rough. He walks ahead twenty, thirty, fifty yards, to an area well past his longest drive ever on this hole. Then he backs up and covers the fifty yards in front of the sandtrap. All the time he talks to himself, about how it felt coming off the clubface, about lateral stances, about any number of things which don't apply, which I know the words for but not their meanings. In all the time he spends looking I don't move; I stand by the sandtrap with my arms crossed. It doesn't take long before the shivering starts.

He hates to lose a ball. It's a matter of honour for him, to find it wherever it has gone, to play it wherever it might be. I've seen him break clubs on rocks, trees, fenceposts. It's like losing a tooth for him, to move on without finding his ball.

The ground is soft and wet from rain and night dew, and so it's easy, when I adjust my foot, to press the ball into the ground. I do it slowly, just with my weight. It takes a long time to really make it disappear, but that is all right, I have plenty of time as Daddy wanders back and forth, sweeping the ground now with his club, his six-iron, his lifesaver.

Probably a half hour later he says, "I wonder if it plugged somewhere?" and I shake my head, I don't know. He takes another ball from his bag, fingers it awhile, as if expecting the first one to call out still. "Oh, well," he says finally, "we'll only play nine holes," and then he swings and stares off into the black and listens, again, for the landing.

FOURTEEN

I live for part of the time in a falling down old farmhouse I bought six years ago, on twenty-five acres of mostly fallow fields and reclaimed bush with a dying apple orchard, about forty-five minutes out of town. I had someone work on the roof when I moved in and re-did the foundation, but I haven't touched anything else: the pipes still vibrate when I turn on the water and the kitchen is insanely small, the windows so old the glass is rippled and you can feel the winter winds right through them. The insulation, what there is of it, is about forty-five years old. It's a good house for staying near the fire and reading with a blanket over your legs and a glass of wine nearby, for listening to the robins who have nested in the bathroom window in the spring, for watching the summer thunderstorms roll in from the west over the brow of the low hills that edge the three front windows of the living room. It's my quiet place, my old place, which I thought I'd be able to retreat to more and more often as the years went by but have found the opposite: the harder I work the more work there is; the faster I move the more afraid I am to stop.

When I bought the place I thought I'd probably tear down the building and create a brand-new "original" farmhouse, with skylights and geothermal insulation, a solarium and loft and a room that would be just for putting the sun to bed. An architect's house. I had the money to do it. It would have been good advertising. I still might do it. When the electrical system goes, I tell myself, or when the plumbing fails completely, or when the worms have got the support beams and it really is time. Everything dies. Re-birth is just a part of life.

I have my condo, which doubles as my office, to turn the heads of clients. I had it done over in bird's eye maple with rugs on the walls and windows on the ceiling and a desk that disappears into an alcove when it's time to entertain. I spent a fortune remodelling. They did a five-page spread on it in *Place* (June 1989), just before the market collapsed. Someday I'll be able to sell it for something approaching what I've spent on it.

It's a guilty pleasure to retreat to the country where the paint is peeling and the porch sags and I haven't even installed a shower in the bathroom much less changed the wallpaper. Out here I feel like a dentist with a secret love of chocolate, a doctor who smokes, an aerobics instructor who can finally let her stomach sag. Away with the business suit, the eyeshadow, the nail gloss, the computerized daytimer in my brief case. On with the sweat pants and the cuddly sweater and the rubber boots for tramping out back where the stream plunges into the woods; there's no sound of traffic and leaves get in your hair. Where I can breathe, and be quiet.

I'm growing tomatoes in the back. They aren't doing very well: I planted them too late and have hardly returned to water them, but in theory they're there. There's a hermit in me who could live here a long time. If I wasn't still paying for my office and my car I would probably do it. That's what's so attractive and frightening about the place. I'm thirty-five. I've never had a lover. I could come here and live like the moss on the rocks in the stream and probably be happy.

"God, it's been ages," Roxanne says. We're having lunch at the Antipasto, which we used to manage every week when she was working, but now it's perhaps twice a year. She has rounded out and looks more grown-up. There's fatigue in the sags beneath the eyes but more light in the pupils. Felice is nearly one and Robert Jr. will be starting kindergarten in two weeks — Roxanne can smell the freedom, it seems so close.

"Things are busy," I tell her. We're drinking our wine and the waiter is late taking our orders. I'm due to meet a client in thirty-two minutes. I should have re-scheduled. I could probably phone him now, or get Janice to phone him, but it's so unprofessional. What's taking so long? The place is hardly busy. I glance at my watch and try to catch the waiter's eye.

"It's so nice, I can't tell you, to just get out and have *lunch*!" Roxanne says, re-opening her menu (a mistake — he'll think we aren't ready to order). Could I re-schedule for Friday? I hate having to bump up other meetings. "I have to get out more, there's no doubt about it," Roxanne says. "You get so socked in with kids. Off to the library, over to the supermarket, home to get lunch, and then when they go to sleep you put the laundry in, and the next thing you know . . . "

"Excuse me, I just have to make a call," I say, and I take my phone out of my briefcase.

"God, Garland," she says, "I didn't know you had one of those. I am *so impressed*."

"Believe me, it's more of a pain than anything else," I say, and press the button for Janice. It rings seventeen times. She's out in the back doing her bloody tai chi. How many times have I told her she *has* to answer the phones at lunch-time? I hang up reluctantly and the phone rings right in my hand. It's my client, saying he's running late — can we do it on Thursday? I give him my best reluctant tone and consult my electronic daytimer which says there's a crack late Thursday afternoon, but did Janice update it? For the thousandth time I swear I'm going back to a hand-written notebook.

"Yes, Thursday's fine," I say, and set the time.

I turn off the ringer and put my phone away. The waiter finally takes my order and I forget that I don't have to be angry at him anymore. I order the veal and ask him how long he thinks it'll be before it's ready.

When he goes Roxanne says, "You've lost a little weight, haven't you?"

"No. Gained if anything," I say.

"You're still doing that aerobics class?"

"No, I stopped," I say. "Something happened this summer — I got insanely busy with that project for the Brotherhood of Maintenance Professionals."

"Who?"

"Oh, it's a union of window washers, as far as I can tell. They've taken over two floors of this crumbling old building off York Street, and they wanted some kind of fountain motif in their lobby. They still haven't paid me for it, now that I think of it." I tell her the long, not terribly interesting story.

"So," she says, when I pause for some wine, "you stopped doing aerobics."

"I just got out of it, I guess. It seems silly in the middle of the summer to be inside a windowless gym sweating like a maniac."

"God, if I only had the *time* to do aerobics," she says. "When the kids are older. That's sort of my mantra these days. 'When the kids are older, when the kids are older.'" She says it in her funny drone. "Robert keeps telling me I should be doing something for myself. He'll pay for it, he says. Yeah, with whose money? We can't afford for me to go out and join fitness clubs. Not if I have to get a sitter at the same time."

The wine and company have their effect. I start to relax a little. Roxanne brings out her pictures. I haven't seen the kids since Robert Jr.'s birthday. Felice has the eyes of a stunning beauty. Roxanne says she reminds her of me, and I say, "Give her a break. I don't think Felice is going to be doomed to a matronly existence."

I say it with my usual tone: *doomed to a matronly existence.* Roxanne has encountered the expression countless times, but this time she takes it more seriously than I mean her to.

"Oh come on," she says. "You've always had to beat men off with a stick. Don't you go on about a *matronly existence*."

"Thank you for your words of encouragement," I say. "It's never too late."

"Well, what's happened with George?" she says. "Wasn't that the fellow you were seeing in the spring?"

"I was never seeing him," I say.

"What do you mean? You went to the opera, you went to that horrible avant-garde theatre piece I remember you telling me about. I couldn't even get you on the phone you were out to dinner so often."

"But we were never going out," I say.

"What was it, then?"

"Well, he was having a hard time after his divorce and I was getting tired talking to myself, so we just started doing things together. That was all. Nothing happened."

"I thought his divorce was six years ago."

Roxanne is amazing in her ability to remember the details of the private lives of the men who show the slightest glimmer of interest in me.

"Divorced men take forever to get over it," I say.

That stops her for a while. She nears the end of her linguini. I know she wants to linger over a dessert, but I'm going to have to disappoint her. If I head back soon maybe I can grab some time to actually do some work.

"So, are you seeing anybody now?" she asks.

"Work has been unbelievable," I say. "You just don't know till you run your own business. I guess it's like having a baby. I'm afraid I'm —"

"But there is somebody who's interested in you," she says, smiling.

"No there isn't."

"Of course there is."

"No, I just told you, I've been such a hermit —"

"There's always somebody interested in you."

"That's not true."

"Ever since I've known you there has always been somebody interested in you, and probably four or five others you just didn't know were interested in you."

Roxanne has this thing about boosting my self-esteem.

"You're blushing. God! I bet he's a younger man!"

"Roxanne — !"

"Now you're completely red. Come on, out with it. You have to get going pretty soon and we aren't going to have lunch again for six months."

"Well," I say, putting my fork down and having a little bit of wine. "There's someone who goes to meditation — I forgot to tell you, I'm going to meditation. He's married. He has a child. And he keeps looking at me like I'm the answer to everything."

Roxanne waits for more. I shrug my shoulders. "That's it!" I say. "It's all a very minor sub-plot. I just got the feeling from the first time he looked at me he was going to ask me out. And a married man has no right to look at a woman like that. Even a matronly one."

"You're sure that he's married?" she asks. "He told you? He's wearing a ring?"

"He's married."

"Lot's of people who look married are divorced these days."

"I'm sure I'm not going to find out." I take her hand, she's looking so confused, so full of advice. "I'm not the romantic type, Roxanne. I wear socks to bed. I can't sleep without them. There's no getting around it." I signal the waiter, who brings the bill in seconds. He must have been waiting to clear the table.

"Anyway, it's been a very nice lunch."

FIFTEEN

The lunch with Roxanne rattles me, makes me wonder what's going on. He's a shadow sneaking into the oddest moments of my thoughts. I turn to pull down a volume on water tables and I'm sure I see him in the corner of my eye, lurking by the doorway, filling the frame in his t-shirt and his ripped jeans and his youth. He knows he's very good looking, which is unsettling, just as it's unsettling to know so little about him. He's married, has a child, and is going to ask me out — that's all I know. He's like an event primed to happen, only I don't know when, and there's nothing to do to prepare myself. The scene runs through my head while I talk to a client, and I can't stop it — my brain divides, and one-half is evaluating construction companies while the other is silently saying, "Well, uh, thank you but no — I don't think I can."

I don't think I can. I don't think I can. The phrase follows me through a microwave dinner, through an hour and half of sitcoms on the television, through two hours and seventeen minutes of lying awake trying not to look at my digital clock. I'm a terrible sleeper, I don't need this shit.

"No, thank you, that's very kind, but . . . I don't think I can." I practise it in front of the mirror, looking down one time, straight into my own eyes the next. "Oh, thank you —" how to fake the surprise? — "but I really don't think —"

The mirror doesn't lie. I look better than I should, after all this time and so little exercise and eating the way I eat. If I only looked the way I'm supposed to look, given my habits, then I wouldn't have this problem of rehearsing in front of the mirror. "Oh, well, thanks, but —"

I get to Alex's, just before seven on the Tuesday — I make sure I'm not early. I carefully keep my eyes down so I can scan the room but not meet anybody's gaze. I just don't want to sit near him. I don't want to encourage him in any way.

But he isn't there. I'm so sure he'll be sitting already, will turn those dark eyes and appear so relaxed and intense and dreadfully interested . . . He said, "I'll see you on Tuesday." Today is Tuesday, but the room is pale. Alex says something pleasant to me and I hardly know what to reply, and then when I'm sitting it takes the longest time to get over it, to have my heart calm down.

Is that it? He's not coming anymore? Is that it?

My back gets itchy, my legs stiffen, my breathing becomes undisciplined. But I fall down the hole eventually, and there she is at the door, my old teacher from grade six, and Dad coming out of the den sheepishly.

"Miss Reynolds!" I say, startled, it's so incongruous to see her here, as if she has come back to tell me I didn't pass my spelling exam after all and will have to re-do my grade six year, starting now.

"It's nice to see you Garland," she says, stretching out her hand and walking through the door, although I've not invited her in. She's wearing very tight, faded blue jeans and a silky, maroon blouse with just a little cotton shirt underneath, no bra, and her hair, which everyone used say they'd kill for it was so glossy, is still beautiful, combed straight down her back all the way to her bum, shining even in the dull light of our hallway. "You've grown up so much," she says.

"Darlene!" Daddy says, wiping his hands on his pants for no reason whatsoever. He squeezes by me in the hall. She leans in his direction, expecting to be kissed — anyone can read the meaning in the motion — but he turns his head at the last moment and takes her purse instead, right off her shoulder. It's such an awkward movement I'd burst into laughter if I wasn't so shocked.

"I'll just . . . I'll take this," he stammers, then, "Come on in! Garland, you remember Miss Reynolds —"

Robbed of her purse, she walks with her hands behind her back, looking around the hall like she's about to take possession. Daddy puts the purse right in the middle of the tiny counter in the kitchen where I'm preparing the liver for tonight.

"What I really wanted to show you was the basement," Daddy says, too quickly.

"Perhaps I could speak to you for a moment," I say to him, every word politely enunciated.

We go into the living room. "Is she coming for dinner?" I ask.

"I thought that, well, maybe —"

"I could have prepared a dinner if you had told me."

"I thought she could just share what we're having. It doesn't matter. Don't take it so seriously."

"We're having liver. We don't even have any bacon. I don't think I have enough for three people."

"Well, we'll go out then —"

"I have a biology assignment due for tomorrow."

"You can do it after we come back."

"I'm going to be up most of the night with it as it is."

"Garland," he says, cupping my cheek in his good hand. "It's only school."

"What do you *mean* it's only school? You don't want me to work very hard, is that it? You don't want me to go to university? You want me to work at Woolworth's or be a waitress or work in some factory somewhere?"

This last remark cuts him I know, but I can't help myself. His hand falls away.

"I just want you to get some fun out of life," he says.

I go ahead and prepare my liver, for one, while they play in the basement. Miss Reynolds's laughter mixes with Daddy's words of praise. "Good shot, yes, but too hard! Watch out — on no! — it's going right off the green!" She's obviously too young for him. She can't possibly be interested in him. Where in the universe could they have met?

When they finally finish their putting play I'm up in my room, eating dinner at my desk, my biology textbook propped open in front of me, my lab book on my lap. The liver has been cooked to leather but even at that is more digestible than "Photosynthesis in Oceanic Vegetation." Miss Reynolds's words carry right up the heating vent as if she were broadcasting them to me on the radio.

"Well, surely she must come. Try her again. I really would like to —"

"She's not taking it very well, Darlene," Daddy says. "She's very private anyway. I think we should just let her get used to it for a while."

"I thought the idea was we would all do something together tonight."

"Another night," Daddy says. "We're going now, Garland!" he calls out, his voice hardly louder than it already was, travelling up the vent. "We won't be too late. Don't work too hard, all right?"

I take another bite of liver and turn the page.

They burn like a fire in the ditch, barely under control. It's dinner on Wednesday, again on Thursday, a movie on Friday but they can't tell me anything about it. Daddy spends Saturday afternoon at "her place," and on Sunday we all go for a drive, me sitting in the back, a reluctant hostage, while Daddy drives and she chatters in peasant dress and sandals, her hair long and free.

"What about your French?" she says, twisting back to establish eye contact. "How's that going? You always had a flair for the language."

"Dropped it," I say.

"Oh good heavens, French is very important."

"Garland's taking three maths and three sciences," Daddy says, twisting back as well. I wonder who's watching the road? "She's going to be an engineer."

"But what about your art? I remember all those horses you used to draw."

I never in my life have drawn a horse. She is remembering two hundred other twelve-year-old girls.

"Actually, there's a painting in the living room," Daddy says, holding up my part of the conversation. "The two old farmhouses. With the sky and everything."

"Oh yes, I remember," she says, too enthusiastically. "That's really very well done. Did you do that, Garland?"

We're heading out of the city, new spring fields whizzing by us in muddy expanses, the first green shadow appearing on the trees.

"Yes, sure, she did that one," Daddy says, picking up for me again. They exchange glances.

She has no idea about him.

We stop for tea at a fancified country place in the little town of Milldown. The restaurant is an old country home fussed over to the point of panic. We're the only customers except for a couple of bikers with long tangled hair and Fu Manchu moustaches smoking cigarettes they've rolled themselves. The tablecloths are chequered red and white and the bikers are black leather and sweat. Miss Reynolds eyes them with too much interest.

As Miss Reynolds adjusts her chair — she wants me to call her Darlene, but I can't — the hem of her long skirt rides up and I notice that she doesn't shave her legs. It only takes a moment to see and then of course I have to wonder — does Daddy know? It's barely a moment more before I think — are they sleeping together? Because if they're sleeping together then he must know. But maybe they do and he doesn't. There's a girl at school, Merriwell Hart, who's sleeping with one of the boys from the hockey team, and she doesn't even know what his thing looks like. It's true, everybody knows because she told Suzanne Lane who has a mouth like a broken gate. She has slept with him at least twice but it was always in the dark and they kept their clothes on (they just rearranged them a bit) and so she never saw, she just *felt*.

Miss Reynolds has herbal tea. Daddy has a cup of coffee. I say I'm not thirsty. The dessert tray comes around and I refuse, saying I'm watching my weight. Miss Reynolds — *Darlene* — says, "Oh come on, don't give me that. You have no weight to watch. It's women like me who are trying to look like *you*."

Why Miss Reynolds wants to look like a flat-chested girl I've no idea.

"You must have the boys just lining up for you," she goes on. "Have you got a boyfriend?"

I consider impaling myself on my fork to get out of this conversation.

"Garland is very serious about her schoolwork," Daddy says.

"Yes, undoubtedly," Miss Reynolds says, digging in as the dessert cart rolls on. "But probably quite a few boys are very serious about her."

Daddy makes a little sign with his eyes, telling her stop, this isn't the right topic. She wants to pursue it. I don't give her the chance. "So how about you, *Darlene,*" I say. "Any interesting men in your life? They must be just about falling over themselves to get in your pants."

It seems a funny remark to me but they don't laugh. A truck goes by outside the window and the bikers get up to leave and I think how wonderful it would be to join them, just walk away and wear black and watch the world spin by.

"Excuse me," I say, finally. "I think I have to go the bathroom."

"That's a good idea," Miss Reynolds says, putting down her tea. "We'll go together."

What does she think, I can't go to the bathroom by myself?

She leads the way, and for the first time I realize I'm just slightly taller than her. For whatever it's worth.

"So we haven't really had a chance to talk," she says, rinsing her face in front of the mirror. I hate it when people say they have to go to the bathroom but don't, really. And what does she mean by talk? She's been talking non-stop since we started out today.

"I guess things have been pretty difficult for you since your mother died."

Like, all my life, you mean.

"I know it's often very difficult when a parent . . . starts to see someone else. I know it can be very disturbing and confusing. You've already lost one parent. That's too much for someone your age to deal with."

What does she think I am, eight years old?

"I really . . . I had no idea he was your father when I met him. I hadn't remembered him at all. Until he mentioned it. Quite late in the game, actually. Garland, why are you looking like that?"

"I have to have a pee, Miss Reynolds!"

"Well then GO, for heaven's sakes!" she says in her grade six teacher's voice.

"You have to be patient with us," she says when I get out. She leans against the counter with her arms folded, the sleeves of her Indian print dress rolled up, her feet crossed at the ankles, as if she's ready to stay here a long time, to get results.

"You have to be patient with us and we'll be patient with you," she repeats. "The thing you have to remember with older people is that, just like you, we're still going through everything for the first time. It's all new to us too. Every single, solitary moment is brand new. We're all learning."

I've no idea what she's talking about.

"You're turning into an extremely beautiful young woman. I'm sure you've been told that more than a few times by now. Is there anyone? Have you started going out with any boys?"

"I think we should get back," I say.

"It's nothing to be ashamed about! Everyone . . . everybody goes through this awkward stage when it's all so fucking new and your hormones are raging around and you get these — what?"

I've never in my life heard a teacher use a word like that. It sounds like the most obscene thing I've ever heard.

"Whatever you and my father do," I say, heading for the door and fresh air, "is your business. It's not my concern. You're both adults. I hardly think you need to consult me."

SIXTEEN

It rains on Thursday. I wake up from a strange dream of waiting at a toll booth but I can never toss my quarter in — I keep missing the basket, till finally I'm out of quarters but I can't open my door to pick up the ones I've dropped, and then there's a line-up three miles long behind me while I search through my purse and count out my pennies: twenty-one, twenty-two, twenty-three . . . aren't there any more?

It's the kind of dream I'd normally be happy to leave, but when I realize I'm awake it seems like too much effort to get up. The air is too heavy. It's too difficult to keep my eyes open, let alone move. If I just go back to sleep I won't be back in the toll booth, I promise. There's too much to do, that's part of the heaviness. I've been running like a crazy woman for weeks and it's all right once I'm up and going, there's momentum there, but when I'm stopped it's like I'm in water, where it's best to just float and breathe.

I turn over. That's possible when you're in water — to turn over and float and conserve energy. Don't think. That's the key. As soon as you start to think you realize you have a client coming at 8:30, and it's now 7:55 by the blurry numbers on the digital clock.

And that's how the day goes, up and running, bolting down a coffee while blow-drying and trying to look at my notes to remember who this person is and what I said I'd do for them.

In the afternoon I rush out to Edwardsville, a town allegedly on the edge of my regional map. There must have been prosperous farms here in some part of the century, but now it's three houses and a closed gas station and no bloody sign, so I pass through it four times before realizing it is the place after all. Process of elimination: I follow all the regional roads fifteen kilometres to nowhere and then turn back. Edwardsville, I deduct, is the centre of nowhere.

When I left the city my gas gauge was comfortably on one-quarter full. I normally can drive a week on one-quarter, but by the time I pull into the abandoned gas station I'm in the red, the needle scraping E.

I slam the door as I get out and wonder which of the three houses belongs to my client. It was somebody who called out of the blue, couldn't really say how he got my name, but he wanted some sort of farmhouse renovation. He couldn't even give me a full address, just the big red house on Regional 16 in Edwardsville. "There's only one red house," he said. Well, I'm here and I see three grey ones, all with aluminum siding so old it looks like it will peel off in the wind.

"There's no red house," I say out loud to the empty winds of Edwardsville.

I'm here, I'm on time despite having to travel every road in the region. I'm practically out of gas and there's no fucking red house.

I go back to my car and whiz through my electronic organizer so I can call the bastard and let him have it straight through the airwaves. To hell with his business, whatever it was, I wouldn't want to touch it with a hundred-foot pole. Give me a break — Edwardsville! I have my phone out, ready to blast him, as I scan the screen for his number.

I didn't enter it. It's unbelievable. I always enter everybody's number.

I phone the office to get Janice to scan the backup, but I know even as I ask her it's not there; nothing is ever in the backup, at least not anything you really need.

The guy phones a little later. He gave me the wrong directions. It's okay, he says; he already hired somebody else. He hangs up.

It's that kind of day. I drive home with the needle below E, past gas station after gas station closed because of the fucking recession. It seems to me I know exactly what's going to happen. I'm going to run out of gas on one of these unmapped backroads and get picked up by a couple of drooling escaped convicts who lurch out of the woods.

The B movie scenes continue running through my head even after I've safely filled up at a brightly lit station on the edge of civilization. I'm in such a mood that when I see an oafish police officer sipping coffee in a cruiser beside the FREE GLASSWARE advertisement I'm sure he's going to pull me over and give me a ticket for just looking at him and thinking these thoughts.

My microwave doesn't work at home. I eat two carrot sticks and throw my clothes off — there! Take that, you stupid body! Fuck it to meditation. Nobody could meditate in the mood I'm in. I have a bath and close my eyes and fall straight away in anger.

"It doesn't matter," I say. "It has nothing to do with me. Why did you even bring it up? It doesn't matter."

Daddy is standing in the doorway of my room. It's one o'clock in the morning and he is skulking in, his shoes in his hands, while I'm up still struggling with the root proof of the quadratic equation.

"If it doesn't matter, Garland, then why are you being so hostile to Darlene?"

"I'm not being hostile. I didn't want to go tonight because I have a major test tomorrow and I can't even remember half the stupid formulas. Most parents would be happy their child was in studying."

"You work too hard," he says, taking a step into the room, which is my space; it makes me uncomfortable to have anyone else here.

"Thanks for the encouragement." I duck my head into the book.

"You have to . . . you can't ignore the social . . . aspect of high school. Of any part of your life, really, it's too . . . unbalanced if you just . . . "

"I'm doing the best I can!" I say and he backs up that step.

"I know honey, I know."

He stands there, not sure what to say. I flip the page over, stare at my notes which might as well be written in Russian.

"You're going to be exhausted in the morning," I say. "Why don't you get your sleep?"

He nods his head stiffly, unwilling to admit defeat.

"Garland, I —"

"You used to *have* something," I say, slamming down my pencil. "Nothing was going to stand in your way and now you're totally distracted —"

"Garland —"

"You had a focus, you had a reason, you had something that was going to set you apart from —"

"Garland!"

"— the others, and what has happened to it? The first *girl* who comes along and all of a sudden you're this —"

"Stop talking for a second!" he says, walking in and shaking me almost out of my chair. "You always knew everything. From the day you could talk you knew everything. Well you don't. Do you understand that? You don't know everything!"

I look up at him till he lets me go, and then I rub my arms where his thumbs were.

"You think you can go through life on your own," he says. "You think it's all one person against the world. Well it isn't. You can't do it. It's not the way we're designed."

"I know you had something you *really* wanted to do, you were aiming for, training for, and now —"

"Trust me," he says, walking back to the door, his head bowed. "You're going to find out sooner or later. It's not the way we're designed."

I look at him. I don't want to cry. Not in front of him.

"I'm only your father, what do I know?" he says.

The phone goes off like a bomb, startling me into the present. It takes a moment to recover, remember where and who I am.

I should just let the machine answer it, but at the last moment I pick it up. "Yes?"

"Hello, is this, uh, is this Garland?"

"Yes."

"I'm sorry for calling so late, maybe this isn't a good time."

It's him. I can hardly believe he's calling me.

"Anyway, it's Jim Kinnell from your meditation class."

"Yes?"

"How are you? I didn't see you in the class tonight, but I guess you normally go on —"

"Tuesdays, yes."

"Anyway, I was talking to Alex this evening, and she mentioned that you're an architect."

I can't believe it.

"She said you help plan a lot of structural renovations."

I cannot believe it.

"Anyway, it's a long story, but my grandfather is getting married, and he's been living with us so long he doesn't really want to move out, so what we're planning —"

He's hiring me to work for him instead of asking me out.

"— is to make a sort of suite for them, a honeymoon suite, my Mom calls it."

"You live with your mother?"

"Yes. And my grandfather too. Anyway, we were wondering —"

"And your little girl."

"And Cedes, yes. But she's not mine. She's just staying with us till Christmas."

"Where are her — ?"

"Well, her Dad was last seen on a bus to Yellowknife. At least that's the story we got. It's very hard to tell with Mirele. But she — Mirele, the mother — is staying at an ashram in India for a while."

"Ah."

"Well, she's an . . . old family friend. She used to stay with us when she was younger. So mostly it's my Mom who's looking after Cedes, who is really much nicer than when you met her. She hadn't had her nap. You know how kids are, they lose it completely."

"Ah." There's a pause while I digest all this family history which he would never have told me if he didn't really mean to ask me out instead of just hire me, like a coward.

"Is there, I don't know, sometime over the weekend that you could come over?" he asks, getting back to business. I'd meant to retreat to the farm, camp in bed with a book for two days.

"Yes, sure, that would be fine," I say, flipping on my organizer and taking down the address.

SEVENTEEN

The house is just on the edge of Ridgewood, one of the quieter, more prosperous neighbourhoods. It's only a few blocks from the Limedale Road, mile after mile of electronics shops, strip malls, burger palaces and convenience stores. But on the other side, the Ridgewood side, are old oaks and blue spruce, and large, comfortable, settled-in houses, and the river further down.

I'm surprised by how small the house is when I get to it, just a bungalow with a couple of dormers upstairs, probably not even the original construction. I hadn't noticed this collection of three, four little houses on the north end of the street; they get lost with so many four and five bedroom battleships around them. (I prefer small houses myself. But then I've never lived in a large family.) There's a nice porch in the front, but the roof needs work.

At the door they're all lined up waiting to meet me. Jim is

first, in loose pants and a sweater, looking nervous; then Mrs. Kinnell, a firm-looking, grey-haired woman in sensible shoes who holds my gaze too long, embarrassing me; then Trafford, the grandfather, enormous (almost as tall as Jim), leaning on a cane so long and black and knotted it looks a part of him, an extension of his reach; and finally Celia, a tiny Scottish woman with lively green eyes, not much older than Jim's mother, the bride-to-be I gather.

"Maybe we can make a little room here," Jim says, like a PA announcer, after I've clasped their hands one by one. They don't make room quickly.

"She's much nicer than the last one," Trafford says, leaning down to Celia and speaking too loud.

"Have you had other architects?" I ask Jim, walking into the living room. He stubs his foot on an easy chair and says, "No, no."

"We're just having tea," Mrs. Kinnell says, so I sit on the edge of the sofa, my briefcase by my feet.

Mrs. Kinnell and Celia melt into the kitchen. Trafford sits in the easy chair opposite me. Jim stands awkwardly, his hands in his pockets.

"So, where did you meet our James, then?" Trafford asks, folding his huge hands together.

"Oh well, I suppose we go to the same meditation class," I say.

"What's that?" he says, leaning forward and turning his head sideways.

"Meditation class, Grandfather," Jim says.

"Is that where you sit and hold your breath and think about what direction the sun is going?"

"Uh, I don't think you're supposed to hold your breath exactly," I say.

"What's that?"

"No, you have to breathe!" I shout, and then turn to Jim. "What's that about the sun?"

"Just what Phil talks about," he says.

"Oh," I say, retreating. Jim is probably one of the ones who actually listens to what Alex's husband says.

"The Western sun is the most dominant in our culture, the evening sun, setting sun. Sophisticated, jaded, cynical." (He speaks louder than normal, trying to include his grandfather in the conversation.) "And the Eastern sun is what we need more of — just that fresh start in the morning, that clear light, a sense of optimism. *Drala*."

"Who?" Trafford asks.

"*Drala*. It's a Tibetan word, it means 'everyday magic.' Bringing a sense of the Eastern sun into the room with you."

"You wouldn't know he's a university professor, would you?" Trafford says, leaning towards me so far I think he's going to fall off the edge of his chair.

"Is that what he is?" I reply.

Tea is ready in a few moments. When the two women arrive, the room suddenly becomes very small. It seems like the last thing they want to discuss is renovations. Finally I turn to Celia and say, "So, I understand you and Trafford are to be congratulated," and she turns pink as a rose under glass, just the way a bride is supposed to. "Wherever did you meet?"

It's just a trick of mine, a conversational device with new clients. Every couple has a story, I've found, and it gets us beyond the weather and a little closer to what they want to do with the house.

"We met at the Sunflower," she says in a Scottish lilt, so soft that Trafford leans in towards her. "It's a recreation centre for us oldies," she says. "I teach a class of Scottish dance on Tuesdays, not too late. There aren't very many men in the class, you understand, so when Trafford arrived a few years ago he was surrounded. But he was an odd man. He wouldn'a dance."

"Couldn'a!" Trafford says, slipping into her accent. "*I was stricken!*"

"He was stricken, the poor lad," Celia says, picking up the refrain. "He couldn'a move his feet."

"I asked her to marry me right then," he says. "I mean when we were alone. She told me I was crazy. I agreed completely."

"So did you eventually learn to dance?" I ask.

"What's that?"

"No, he's still stiff as a board," Celia says, softly, but Trafford understands her completely, nodding his head.

"I kept coming back till she agreed to have dinner with me!" he says. "It took two months!"

"I finally agreed just to get him off my back."

"And that was history!" Trafford pronounces, reaching across to hold her hand. She looks so tiny beside him, and yet so completely in control.

"Kinnell men fall like a ton of bricks!" he says, turning to me. "But I suppose you already know that!"

"Trafford!" Mrs. Kinnell says, poking his leg. "*What?*" he says, turning back to her. "Grandfather!" Jim says, looking ready to dump tea all over him.

"I'm just noting the obvious!"

It's a peculiar situation. I concentrate on my tea. Then there's a noise from the doorway into the kitchen.

"Mommy?" the little girl says, clutching a blanket to her cheek, her hair rumpled with sleep. She looks straight at me.

"No, honey," Mrs. Kinnell says, half-rising, but the girl puts her head down and runs for me. I only have a second to safely place my tea on the side table before she buries her face in my blouse.

"Cedes," Jim says, kneeling beside her, stroking her tangled, little girl hair. "Remember this is the lady I told you was going to . . . "

"I thought Mommy was coming home," she says, still clutching me.

"Yes, she is honey. But not right now. Later. Around Christmas."

She's got a real grip for someone so young. I pull her up onto my lap.

"Were you sleeping?" I say to her, brushing a tear from her cheek.

"I was with Christie and Lu Chun. And there were cows there too."

I look up to Jim for help.

"The Olympic skaters," he says. "And she always dreams about cows."

"Ah." Is this the same girl who was so bratty in the parking lot? She refuses to leave my lap, so I carry her through the inspection tour of the upstairs where the honeymoon suite is to go. Everyone comes along.

"What I was thinking of . . . what *we* were thinking of —" Trafford says, putting a protective arm around his tiny Celia.

"There's no need to shout, Trafford," she says.

"*What?*"

They want to open up the upstairs, tear down the walls between the two smallish bedrooms and then build an extension out over the garage which will comprise, mostly, an enormous bathroom.

"It has to be huge!" Trafford says, spreading his arms wide.

"Quite large," Celia says, holding his hand.

"The bedroom?" I ask.

"No, no, the bathroom," she says, sliding her tongue over

the word till it comes out "rhume." "All my life I've dreamed of enjoying a more than adequate bath-rhume."

"You want a Jacuzzi?"

"Big as we can get!" Jim says.

"I'll have to look at the support beams in the garage," I say. "You might have to replace them."

"Ay, we will, we will!" Trafford says, almost gleefully.

"Whatever it costs," Celia says. "But can you see what we want, Garland?"

I take some notes and measurements, then some pictures with the camera I always bring, and receive several roles of old blueprints they've put together for me. Then we head out to the garage where the news is bad. There's significant rotting along the side beams as well as the roof. The renovations are probably going to cost half as much as the house is worth in this depressed market.

When I tell them they are thoughtful. I expect them to call it off or at least scale things down. I've seen it happen enough with clients. You start with the big dream, and then you work with the practical.

"You could take the money and what you can get for the house and probably buy what you're looking for in a better neighbourhood," I say.

"But then we wouldn't be in this house," Mrs. Kinnell says, as if quoting a Commandment.

"I think we want to stay in this house," Jim says.

"Well, as long as money isn't a problem." I look at them. I don't know anybody for whom money isn't a problem.

"We'll need an estimate," Trafford says.

"Yes. Of course."

There are times when my life feels like it belongs to someone else, when there's a gap between what's happening and what I feel, like a sound lag in a poorly-filmed movie. I'm sitting by the fire in my farmhouse with the lights off, October outside, pressing in black against the window. I drink wine most nights by myself. Does that make me an alcoholic? Only a few glasses. Just the red. It slows me down, uncurls my toes.

I won an academic prize in university, the Doleman Award for Excellence in the School of Architecture. It was for marks only; there wasn't a design competition involved. The prize took four years to achieve. It was won in very slow increments, night after night in the library or at the drafting table. Weekend after weekend of not going out, of not dating, of not having anything else to do, or wanting anything else to do. I remember thinking, sometime in second year, that it would be glamorous to win the Doleman. Glamorous for someone else, actually. For me life's a steady pull, one step then another. For someone else to walk up in mortar and robes, to shake hands with the Dean and turn to squint at the lights, that would be glamorous. But when I was the one all those eyes turned towards, then it felt like some actor was in my body while I floated a few feet away. Not me. The applause didn't apply to me.

The wine slides down my throat as I think, and somehow I think of my first period, at fourteen, late of course. I was in the habit of getting up early in the morning, maybe because Dad was on the early shift then, I can't remember. I used to do my homework, my extra reading, at my desk while nibbling toast. My lamp was a bit like the firelight here; I loved working at that desk. I curled my legs up in my big padded chair, and right in the middle of *To Kill a Mockingbird*, when Atticus is shooting that rabid dog in the street, there was something wet on my nightie and I felt to see if I'd spilled my tea, thinking, "This is odd, I didn't even make tea this morning."

And then I knew exactly what it was. "There," I thought. "Finally I am alive."

Two of the strangest thoughts to have back-to-back: "This is odd, I didn't even make tea this morning," and then, "There, finally I am alive." I brought my hand up and looked at the blood. Then I washed up and went to the closet where I'd kept a package of tampons for two years. I changed, put in a laundry, and never said a word to anyone.

"Finally I am alive." It felt like it then, all day. I'm not sure I've felt it since.

I take another sip of wine and when I close my eyes his are right there, looking in their way boyish and deadly serious, and his hair is curling down his strong neck. He's a beautiful man, it occurs to me.

He's there the next Tuesday. It feels like the easiest thing in the world to catch his gaze when I walk in. It has been a good day anyway. The cheque finally arrived from the Brotherhood of Maintenance Professionals, and the School of Architecture called asking if I would adjudicate a design contest. Funny that I'd just been thinking of them over the weekend. Did I think about them because they were thinking about me, or did they think about me because I was thinking about them? Or is this all an accident? Just like it's an accident that the seat beside Jim is open when I walk in, and we're both a few minutes early, so I can say to him even before hello, "I haven't finished yet, but I'm getting there. I'll have a computer model for you in a couple of days."

I squeeze his leg as I sit down. Then when I take my hand away I pretend I was only trying to steady my balance.

I say hello to Alex who compliments me on my blouse, from Guatemala, a deep red and green and purple pattern, hand-sewn. I normally just wear my sweatsuit to meditation but decided to throw this on, along with a pair of black stretch pants I hardly ever wear. They seemed like the right thing to wear although they make me feel a little exposed.

"I'm sorry to throw you to my family like that," Jim says. "They're a bit much to take, I know."

"Not at all. They're very interesting. And interested, I'd say."

It's a reckless thing to say and Jim fields it shyly.

"They kind of over-react whenever —" he says, clearing his throat. He doesn't finish the thought, but looks down at his crossed legs.

"Your grandfather said you're a professor," I say. Be careful, be careful. But the moment seems shining, bullet-proof.

"Well, he sort of over-reacts about that too," he says. "I teach a course at the college. Just as a sessional. The pay is pretty bad. But I've been doing it for two years, and there will be some full-time positions opening up, maybe after Christmas."

"What do you teach?"

"Oh, well, I did my master's in literature," he says, a little puffed, then smiling self-deprecatingly. "But I teach business writing. To nurses."

I can see a whole roomful of them, in their starched whites, gazing up at their tall young lecturer.

"Why do nurses need to learn business writing?"

"So I can get a paycheque," he says, grinning.

There's more to say, but there are also other people in the room, and Alex starts us off. As we cross legs and straighten our backs and clear our thoughts (mine are too tangled; they can't possibly be cleared), I'm aware of the very few inches between his knee and mine and how long his fingers are, resting there, and how long it takes him between breaths; I seem to draw two for every one of his. They are silly thoughts; I try to amend them.

He's wearing some kind of scent — aftershave? There's just a trace of it. I haven't noticed it before. And he's very clean shaven for seven o'clock in the evening. And his fin-gernails are well-kept, clean and regular, clipped and filed. I can tell just through the slits of my eyes which are supposed to be closed, but there will be no memory-holes tonight. Still, I think of Dad because he used to tell me to be careful about men who didn't take care of their fingernails. What was it he used to say? "It's an indicator of character, Garland. A man who doesn't take care of his fingernails isn't tuned into the little things. You want a man who's tuned into the little things."

"I don't want a man," I say, and there, it's as easy as that, the hole is open and I've fallen in.

"You will. Not now, of course, you're young. But some-time you will. And when you do, check how he keeps up his fingernails."

(The conversation is somewhere in space, empty of con-text, framed like a painting of Dad holding up his own battered hands, his middle stump as ugly and discoloured as ever. The fingernails he has left are perfect.)

Perfect as the day now as the scene shifts to July and a high sun and a blue too full for Daddy and his golf; it seems out of context. He's much better in high winds, hail, snow, darkness, his normal elements of practice. But now the air is too still, the sun too hot, the game too slow and comfortable. He hasn't prepared for this it occurs to me as I watch him warming up on the first tee. Everything is too perfect. He'll have no idea what to do.

It's the district qualifying tournament for A class players.

The qualifying is for the regional qualifying tournament which will be for the provincial, et cetera. Daddy wants to be national amateur champion. He has stayed away from playing tournaments for a long time so that he'll be brilliantly prepared for playing tournaments now. It's all part of the programme. Somehow when he explains it everything makes sense, like when he explains the mechanics of the backswing and the weight distribution on fairway bunker shots. It has something to do with the fact that a watched kettle never boils. Go away, do something else, take the path less travelled. Then when you come back the pot will have boiled, and you'll be ready to be champion. It's all part of the programme.

What's not part of the programme, has never been as far as I know, is Miss Reynolds, Darlene. She's here in her tight faded blue jeans and a halter top and sunglasses that make her eyes look like pink insects. Everyone is looking at her, especially Daddy, who can't seem to decide whether he's a knight preparing for a joust or a golfer trying to tee off. There's just a small group of us watching but we might as well be an audience of millions on TV, he seems so nervous.

He's the first in his group to hit but he can't get his tee in the ground. He bends down once, twice, a third time, but each time the ball falls off and the tee slumps over. I almost go across the rope and do it for him. Finally he gets it right but he's rattled. His warm-up routine is hurried and jerky. Darlene cheers too loudly when he approaches the ball; he looks at her and smiles, petrified, but doesn't start over like he should.

He hits the ball somewhere and Darlene cheers, but there's no other sound except the crunch of wood a few seconds later. He's in the forest, whether on the left or right I don't know, the trees are thick on both sides. Wherever, it's an awful place to be and Daddy returns to his bag. He looks up as the three others hit perfect ones, you can tell by the way they linger to watch their shots, then make little self-satisfied critical noises so that we know they're too good to ever be happy. Then Daddy tees up another one, a provisional, and a few seconds after his swing is greeted again by the crunching sound of trees.

It's a horrible moment. He has to tee up a third and take out an iron to play safe, to make sure he's on the fairway at least. He swings like he's trying to walk the ball out to safe ground; there's no verve, no snap, no rip on the chain. You have to treat this like a dance, I want to tell him — just his own words back at him. You can't dance in a straightjacket. You have to let it go, be spontaneous, trust your body to make the right moves.

He's safe, evidently. Safe but terrified. With the penalty strokes he has taken five shots already, is one over par and over two hundred yards still to the hole and panicked. Instead of his four-wood he takes out his six iron, his safety club, and then even with that squibs it along the ground. I've seen him hit better shots one-handed. In the snow! The world is collapsing and all he can do is stand there and watch.

"You've messed him up completely," I hiss at Darlene who hardly even knows he's playing badly, she's so clued out. I don't wait for a reply, but flee down the fairway to the car because I don't have to be here, I don't have to watch the world self-destruct.

(Alex is calling us out. Is that an hour already? But I can't go. Not now. There's still more.)

"Well anyway, it was a lovely walk," Darlene says. I've driven home and worked on vector analysis and then come back to get them. "They really keep these golf courses in wonderful shape. Do they use pesticides on the grass, darling?"

Daddy, putting his clubs in the trunk, doesn't seem to hear. "Your father started hitting the ball much better after a few holes," she says. "He was hitting it so far I could hardly see where it went. And there was that one hole you putted it in from right out of the long grass. Do you remember that one, darling?"

He nods vaguely, then sits in the back seat in silence like a piece of luggage.

"And the other players were very nice. They really complimented a lot of your shots, didn't they?" We both look back. His eyes are dull, like that day I drove him from this parking lot in winter, nearly frozen.

Even Darlene shuts up when she sees him like this. I put the car in gear and back out.

The problem is Darlene, obviously. On the drive home I have it all worked out. She has distracted him from the one thing he has ever wanted to do. He has been so single-minded all these years, and now that he's finally ready she comes along and throws him off. It's a game of concentration. How many times has Daddy told me that? The really great players have the shot fully developed in their imaginations before they swing. A distracted player can barely hit the ball.

When I steer the car into the driveway, I know the solution. She has to go. Daddy has to tell her. He must clear his thoughts. I've seen him so many times drive himself to train in the worst of conditions. Who kept going despite losing two fingers? Who worked even harder? Who became a better player? Now he has to keep going. Give her up. Focus on what's most important.

When he gets out he doesn't take his clubs out of the car. A good sign, I think, because it means he'll go out later and practise. This is only a minor setback. It's all in the programme.

But when he walks to the door with us, he seems like a much smaller man. He doesn't even wait for me to be out of earshot but turns to Darlene and says, "Let's go to bed."

I can't believe it. My ears burn. She brushes past me, takes his hand as I open the door. And they do it, right upstairs in Daddy's bed, in the afternoon, with Darlene's stupid moans and Daddy grunting and the door left open for God's sake.

"It's okay, it's all right, it's okay," she says to him again and again as I flee the house.

EIGHTEEN

"Just come out of it slowly," Alex says, her hand on my shoulder as I open my eyes. I'm startled for a moment to see her, and then there's Jim kneeling by me. Everyone else has gone.

"Oh, I'm sorry," I say, catching myself, holding Alex's wrist for a moment.

"It's all right," she says.

"I heard you call the time. I just . . . there were a few more things."

"It's fine."

But neither of them is looking at me like it's fine. I stretch my legs, take a quick look at my watch. Eight-thirty. I stayed sitting an extra half hour.

"There's no problem," Alex says. "I just wanted to make sure you were all right. Sometimes people get really . . . "

"No, it's nothing."

"I have some tea made," she says. "Would you like to stay? The both of you?"

I beg off, scramble for my coat and gloves. God! I know some people go over-time. I see them there still sitting as I'm leaving, even after I've stayed to chat with a few of the others. This is the first time it has happened to me.

"I know I really have to . . . to work on clearing my thoughts," I say to Alex at the door. Jim is hovering behind me.

"Well, thoughts are just thoughts," she says. "Sometimes you can't clear them away till you can see where they're going."

"Sometimes they're just going backwards," I say, stepping through the doorway. The night has turned cold. Almost winter. I put my hands over my ears as I walk away.

"I don't know how people can function in this kind of weather without a hat," I say. "My ears freeze in a minute. I'm a real wimp in the winter."

Jim offers a wool earband from the pocket of his jacket. I take it.

He has waited an extra half hour for me, and now he's walking along beside me even though I haven't the slightest idea where I'm going.

"Did you ask if I wanted to go for a coffee?" I say. It's a dark street. The street lights seem far apart.

"No," he says.

"Oh. I thought you had."

"Would you like to go for a coffee?"

"I thought you'd never ask," I say.

It takes about twenty minutes to find a place. We walk down Leland Road which should by all rights have three coffee shops to the block, but this particular stretch is mostly stores selling used radio parts, vacuum cleaners and electric motors. I get Jim to tell me about Celia.

"I think she reminds my grandfather of someone from his youth," he says. "He was hopelessly in love with a young woman named Colleen, who talked a mile a minute, apparently, and always kept Grandfather on his toes. She also rejected him, which he never forgot, and never forgave her for either, I think."

"Celia seems very soft-spoken to me," I say.

"Oh, yes, but she can argue her way through anything he says. Which is exactly what he needs. He's been turning into a deaf old buzzard."

"Is she a widow?"

"For twenty-five years. She's the one bringing the money to these renovations. Grandfather's been broke for a long time. He didn't ask her, she just insisted. That's the kind of person she is. Soft exterior, ironwood core. Her first husband was an engineer with the mint. So there's that in common with Grandfather anyway."

"Your grandfather worked for the mint?"

"He was a naval engineer." And Jim tells me the whole story of Trafford's career, and while he's talking we finally find Zero's Donuts, neon light reflecting off the stretches of empty racks where donuts used to be and presumably will be again in the morning. They still have some coffee, old with grounds in it. At least the place is warm. We get a booth by the window. Most of the others in the shop look like they have no other place to go.

"I wouldn't come here alone," I say. "Isn't that a terrible thing to say about our society? As a grown woman I'd feel afraid to walk into this place alone at night."

"What was it you were thinking about?" Jim asks, sipping his coffee as if he doesn't want to drink too much, but he has bought it, after all.

"What?"

"In the meditation. For so long."

"Oh, nothing," I say too quickly.

"It's okay. We don't have to talk about it."

I look down at my coffee. It's such a stupid thing to be hung-up on.

He says, "The only reason I started coming to these meditation classes is that I found sometimes, when everything was right, and my thoughts were cleared or whatever, I mean, they're never really cleared, are they? Maybe for some near-god in India who doesn't need to be part of this world anymore, maybe someone like that can really clear his thoughts. But I found there were times I could get my really best memories of my father. A couple of weeks ago I remembered playing hockey with him. He'd go out with me sometimes on Saturday mornings to the outdoor rink by the park near the river. Really early, before anybody else was there. You know how your fingers nearly freeze in the cold as you sit on the snowbank trying to do up your skates? And then finally you get going and everything is numb you're so cold, but after ten minutes of racing up and down you're so hot you want to take your jacket off?"

"My father didn't play hockey," I say. "Neither did I. But I know what you're talking about."

"Do you?"

I nod.

Jim says, "He taught me how to skate backwards, how to deke out a goalie, how to raise the puck, how to take a pass. He was a marvellous player. He was Junior A when he was young. He could have played in the NHL."

"What happened?" I ask. My coffee is almost finished, but I nurse it along.

"Well, maybe not the NHL," Jim says, smiling. "He was pretty small. Surprising, because Grandfather is so big. He met my Mom when he was twenty. He became a roofer. He died when I was twelve. I never once stepped on a hockey rink again after that."

"Your father died?" I ask. I'd assumed there had simply been a divorce.

"Yes, he did. An aneurism," he says, almost defensively.

"You daydream in meditation, and your father died when you were young," I say.

He looks at me, confused.

"My mother died very soon after I was born," I say. "I thought I was the only one who went on memory-trips in meditation. I was raised by a golf fanatic who used to play in the snow. He didn't have enough sense to play hockey. He lost two fingers and two toes falling through the ice on a water hazard in the middle of January."

"What?"

"Yes!" I say, and I tell him, a story I've never told anyone else, it always seemed too ludicrous to admit. I barely get finished when Jim tells me about Trafford coming to live with them after his father died, and how his mother fell in love later on with a cabinet-maker, and how jealous Trafford was. So I have to tell him about Darlene and my father, and he tells me about his own mother and father, and how Trafford wouldn't even speak to them, they were so much in love. It's one of those evenings, every story leading to another and another, like we're pulling a long chain out of black water hand over hand.

One coffee won't do. A fresh pot is made, thank God, and then the donuts start filling the shelves again, not a moment too soon because I'm getting hungry. We have several, the talk bubbling all the time. I tell him about finding out about mother in the microfilm section of the library in university, and I tell him something else I've never told anyone. "It was like looking up and seeing a star flash by, whoosh, gone! Only you know it was something that happened centuries ago, and the light is just reaching you now, and that's a big part of what's so sad." Then he tells me about dumping his father's ashes in the river and watching the grey powder sink, too heavy to float away.

"I used to sit up on top of our roof at night," he says, "because I thought it was the place where I'd be closest to him, the place where he worked. I thought, you know, if I were ever to see his ghost, it would be there."

"I never wanted to see my mother's ghost," I say, shivering a bit at the thought. "You were lucky. You have some memories of your father. All I have is a photograph. She's kind of turning her head away. Black and white. Daddy wouldn't tell me anything about her."

When I look at my watch it's two o'clock in the morning.

"Oh God! I have to work tomorrow," I say, getting up. "I've really gotten carried away!"

"Is it late?" he asks, then shakes his head when I show him the time.

"How did you come? Did you drive here?" he asks.

"Yes, but my car is back by Alex's."

And so he walks me back, the cold sheeting through me, making me feel giddy and brittle.

He puts his arm around me as we're walking. It catches me by surprise. He's so much taller than I am and the gesture is unexpected. I'm about to move away but he starts rubbing my side to warm me up. "You're shivering," he says.

"I'm a real wimp when it comes to winter," I say, leaning closer because it feels good.

We finally come to my Volvo, sulking a little in the shadows. I have trouble getting the key in the lock. My fingers won't move properly. Jim takes the keychain from me, unlocks the door.

"Did you bring a car tonight?" I ask him. "Or can I give you a lift?"

"It's okay. I'll just run," he says.

"Oh, Jim, it's miles to your house! Are you kidding? I'll just zip by."

"No, thanks. I didn't have a workout today. I'm too hyped anyway. I'll never get to sleep."

"Too much coffee," I say.

"Not just that," he says and then he leans down and kisses me, just like that. And not a little kiss, either.

"I wish you hadn't done that," I say.

"Do you?"

"Yes!"

"Why?" he says, his eyes wide in real question.

"Well, if I have to tell you —"

Before I can finish he has kissed me again and then backed off.

"I'll call you tomorrow," he says and then he turns and, yes, runs off, his arms pumping, his sneakers flashing white in the night, his fist raising now and again as he yowls like a wolf in the canyon of this street.

NINETEEN

He phones in the morning at a quarter to nine. My skull feels like it's been thinned into an eggshell, nearly broken by the jolt of my telephone.

"I just wanted to tell you that I didn't sleep at all last night," he says, too cheerfully. "How about you?"

"Yes I did, thanks," I say, my fingers on the closed crescents of my eyes. "You got back all right?"

"I was fine. It was very good. It probably took me about twenty minutes."

"So you're a runner?" I say. "I mean, you train and all that?"

"Yes. Sometimes."

God! Imagine it. I say, "I don't run at all. I hate physical exercise. I don't like to sweat."

"What do you do?"

"I go for walks. I like to smell flowers. You have to stop a lot to do that."

"That's okay," he says. "Will you have dinner with me tonight?"

"I might fall asleep over dessert."

"I'll catch you before you get chocolate on your face."

"I hate chocolate."

"How can anybody hate chocolate?"

"It has to be lemon meringue."

"I'll catch you before you hit the lemon meringue."

"That's a deal," I say, and then when it's arranged we say we're going to hang up but we don't. We stay on, our talk forming into clever little crystals as we speak, like snow at the flake factory before it has been released, the ideas perfect and unique and gone in an instant, melted into something else.

When I put down the phone the eggshell feeling has left but I recognize the bloating as I walk. My period, which you could normally set your calendar by, has come a week early.

He doesn't own a car, so I pick him up. Mrs. Kinnell at the door looks at me in a queer way. It occurs to me that Jim has told her everything we talked about last night, and then I think no, this is just the way parents look at members of the opposite sex who have come to the door calling for their child, grown or not. And then I think maybe I'm looking at her in a queer way too. Is this the woman who had that fling with the cabinet-maker?

"I worked on it today. I won't have much chance tomorrow but after that I'll probably have something to show you. How are you, Mrs. Kinnell?" I ask.

"Well, not as busy as you," she says cheerfully.

Jim is tying his shoes in the living room. When he disengages himself he keeps rising and rising. It's odd to watch him. He's so tall I expect him to be more awkward. He gives me a big smile. He's wearing a shirt and tie and the same tweed jacket he wore that day in the supermarket. His teaching attire? He hurries to the side table and brings me a bouquet of assorted flowers, extravagantly colourful, redolent of spring. I make the appropriate noises, and it's several more embarrassing moments before we are safely in the car.

"Are you okay?" he says, settling in beside me, bulky in his fall coat.

"Fine."

"You don't like the flowers?"

"They're fine."

"You said you liked flowers."

"I love flowers," I say.

"Oh."

I look at the key in the ignition, my gloved fingers ready to turn.

"You don't like the attention," he says. I look at him, those eyes so intent.

"I want to kiss you," he says.

"I have make-up on."

He kisses me anyway. It's not what I expect. It's never what I expect.

"Next time I won't make such a fuss," he says, drawing back to look at me again. And then I put my hand at the back of his head and we kiss again.

We go to the Antipasto, the restaurant where I have my occasional lunches with Roxanne. The truth is I don't eat out all that often — lunch is usually an apple and a sandwich from the cafeteria across the street and dinner is something frozen I nuke in the microwave and eat at a frantic pace, I'm usually so hungry. Probably savages eat better than I do, but there you go. Thoughts are just thoughts, as Alex says. I'll extend the same consideration to eating patterns. About once a year I buy some book that tells me everything in life comes down to nutrition and I'm damned to rot in a cancer ward for my lack of care. Life seems more normal to me when the sky is falling.

My thoughts whirl and I nearly ding the car as I'm parking it, telling Jim about a professor I had whose cue cards crumbled into dust one day on his desk as he took them out, and he stood there shocked, as if after thirty years of repeating the same lectures he was now going to forget what to say.

"Oh, come on!" Jim says, "the cards actually turned to dust in front of the class?"

"Well, not dust really," I reply, bumping into a post even as I look back at the car I just missed. It's not serious. But I'm a much better driver than this.

"Oh," he says, then, gently, "careful."

"I mean one of them folded and cracked right there in his hand, and some dust did fall out of the card box when he picked it up, so it looked like everything was crumbling into dust. He couldn't get the class to stop laughing."

It's a jumpy, out-of-control evening. I order and then forget immediately what I said I'd have and have to wait for it to arrive before I realize what it is. Fettucini alfredo. Jim has a big plate of plain spaghetti and meatballs. I order a bottle of red wine and then find that Jim doesn't even drink.

"You're kidding," I say. Is he old enough? But he doesn't make a big deal out of it. "I just never got in the habit," he says.

"Well, I like a glass of red wine," I say, and before the evening is out have finished the bottle. But it's over a long period and my head is clear. I tell him things from school I've hardly thought since they happened. Like staying in the library once till after midnight, long after closing, because an assignment was due and I was going to be up all night with it anyway. No one came by to check, and the emergency lights stayed on by my carrel, hidden in the stacks, and it was like I was drifting in space, exploring, free. Then leaving and walking in the dark with the night so still and seeing a light on by the window in one of the student houses, second floor, curtains open, two people kissing.

Jim tells me about a night hitchhiking in Scotland, with the rain pouring down and his wallet nearly empty, trying to get back to the airport to catch his flight, and some old man finally picking him up and giving him something to drink and how when he woke up the roof of the vehicle seemed to be coming off and the sky was opening up, and he could feel a billion stars looking down on him. "There are times like that when everything seems to line up, and it's not that you understand more than usual, it's more, you get a glimpse into how much you don't understand."

Yes, I nod, and he scans my eyes, intent on seeing whether I've known nights like that myself. I try to look like I have. Then he throws me off-balance again, says something I've heard from others but it's never pierced me before, so it sounds new. He says, "You are so very beautiful," and reaches across to take my hand. We're on coffee, and it's late, but I don't want to know the time.

"You say that beautifully," I say, moving my hand away. "I bet you use it often."

"Not so often," he says.

"But you've said it before."

"Perhaps."

And then I say the words I want to retract immediately afterwards. "Cedes's mother?"

He looks away.

"Yes. Mirele."

"So Cedes *is* your daughter?"

"No," he says, as if he really wished she were. "Mirele was someone I knew when I was in school," he says. It's okay. I don't need to know more. But I've started him and it's an evening for truthful talk, for carrying through.

"Mirele came from a diplomatic family, and she travelled around a lot. For a while, when she was young, she used to talk about being struck down like dengue fever — it was a saying she had. I never found out what dengue fever was. I suppose I could look it up. But for a long time I've imagined it must affect you a lot like Mirele, sort of lurking inside your vital organs, staying dormant most of the time, and then when you think that's it, it's over, you break out in a cold sweat and can't sleep." He says it quietly, as if knowing where it's leading but unable to stop.

"That night hitchhiking in Scotland. That was the end of a disastrous trip I took trying to find her. She'd sent me a card, saying she was in St. Andrews, and was getting married, and I thought if I went to her, if I just showed up then . . . "

He stares for a moment at nothing, and smiles slightly. "Anyway, I thought I was cured after that. I just, I went back to school, I dated a few people, a lot of time went by, I started working."

"And then she came back?"

"Yes. But before I get to that, what I was going to say was that no one electrified me the way she did. In a way it was a relief. It was painful to be so hopelessly, frantically turned on by someone. But after it was like going into winter for years. You get used to it. Everything happens in a low gear. You think grey is a normal colour."

"And then she came back."

"I was away at the time, canoeing up north by myself. It was actually very stupid because I'm not a seasoned canoeist, and I got lost a few times, and there were a couple of wild nights when storms came in and I got drenched. I was lucky I didn't get sick. I let my beard grow." He smiles, stroking his cheeks, now smooth. "I was pretty bushed when I got out. Talking to myself, you know, suspicious of strangers. But there were a lot of tranquil times too. It was really worth it. We should go next summer." He looks at me to see if his invitation has registered. "Anyway, when I got back Cedes was in our house. Mirele and my mother always got along well. Mom promised just to look after the girl for a few months."

"So you didn't see Mirele?"

"No."

"How did it feel?"

"It felt manageable," he says, carefully. "At first I wanted to fly to India and find her. Of course, if I couldn't find her in Scotland how was I supposed to find her in India? Anyway, I didn't have the money, and the feeling passed much quicker than I thought. And then —"

"What?"

This time he does find my hand. "Well then I met you," he says, in a way that is not smooth at all but open, like a fresh wound.

"Am I your salvation from dengue fever?" I ask.

"I don't know," he says, and it's me avoiding his eyes this time. "I don't know this feeling. It's very new."

"Not electric?"

"Yes, that. But not a fever. My heart gets very still when I am with you."

The waiter interrupts, noisily stacking chairs on other tables.

"I'm sorry. I've talked too much," he says. "I've made things heavy."

"Well, I asked you," I say, and then we wrestle over the bill. I know he has very little money. I don't mind paying. He insists. I insist.

We split it. I drive him home. Lights are on, his family waiting up. Obligatory words come out — "wonderful time," "thanks so much" — but it feels like we've lost something, are stumbling to find it. His hand is on the door handle. The motor is still running, my foot is on the brake. He doesn't say, "I'll call you tomorrow." He doesn't lean in to kiss me.

He opens the door.

I say, "I've never made love to anybody in my whole life, Jim."

He closes the door. "Why not?"

Because it does not apply to me, I think instinctively. But what actually comes out is, "Because I've *always* been winter inside." I turn off the motor.

He looks at me for a long time. I'm uncertain what he sees.

"I'll call you in the morning," he says, and leans in to kiss me.

TWENTY

"I know you think I'm a failure," Daddy says. It's a strange time, some hours after we normally have our dinner but we haven't eaten. Darlene has just left. It's the first snow of the season and Daddy is standing in my doorway, the snow in the landing window behind looking like it should be hitting his head. I look up from my books. There's never an end to them. There are always more books, more notes to take, more formulae to memorize and reproduce. I'm good at it, the whole game, and so there will always be more.

"I know you think I've given up. Just the way you look at me. You don't have to say a word."

I don't say a word. It's the easy way of surviving. Don't say a word and the day will pass into night. One step will follow another till I'm free. It won't be so long now.

"I want to tell you that Darlene means a lot to me. I can't tell you more than that. I've lived a lot longer than you, so I know some things that you don't, but the thing is, I can't tell you. You wouldn't even believe me. You're eighteen, you think you know everything. Well, you know everything in school. But here's something you don't know. School isn't life. It hardly has anything to do with life. Life is . . . "

He scratches his belly, as if the answer is there. He's getting fat since he stopped his training.

"Life is wilder than you think. That's the thing they don't teach you in school. They make you think life is some tame thing, that it's like being on the line, bolt those fenders, spray that paint, everything happens on time, within quality control. At ten-fifteen you take a piss, have a coffee and a smoke. Or life is reading some book and answering questions and when you're finished you get an A and you go onto another book. But life isn't that. There are forces we can't ignore, that we're part of. You see, I'm trying to tell you but I can't. You have to go through it yourself, to nearly drown before you realize. I want to tell you so you won't miss out."

"You dragged me I don't know how many times out in the snow, in the night, in the wind, in freezing weather, to do your training, to follow your programme, for how many years? And then you have one bad tournament and that's it, you stop everything? That's what I see. It doesn't have anything to do with life, or whatever you're talking about!"

"Sometimes the answer," he says, "is not what you think it is. Sometimes the line is not straight. Sometimes the question is not what you think it is."

I don't know what to say to him when he starts talking like this. Has he been drinking?

"We aren't designed to stand alone," he says. "It's taken me years and years to rediscover this basic fact. Since your mother died, I've been trying as hard as I could to stand alone. But we're not designed for it. The parts wear out. The engine over-heats. The electrical system goes screwy. No matter how hard we work at it we're not complete. That's what I'm trying to tell you, only you're probably just going to insist on figuring it out for yourself."

"What's this got to do with golf?"

The question stops him for a moment.

"I used to write poetry," he says. "I know you won't believe me. But when I was young I wrote poems for your mother which she loved. They're gone now. I threw them out. They weren't very good. But there was one she liked very much. I hardly remember anything of it now, just a couple of lines. 'There comes a time to join the dance, when excuses will not do.' That's all I remember. There's going to come a time when you'll know why she liked that. Not now, but sometime, when the wildness of things has caught up with you. Because it will. 'There comes a time to join the dance.' Will you remember that I told you that?"

"I think I should make some dinner, Dad."

"'There comes a time . . . '"

"Yes I know," I say, getting up and putting my arm around him to get him moving. He *has* been drinking. And he's getting fat and small at the same time.

"It's not a straight line." He weaves a little on the stairs so that I grip him harder, making him laugh. "You don't realize it yet, but sometime you will," he says, clumping to the bottom.

TWENTY-ONE

"I'm just presenting some options," I say as I set up my laptop on the dining room table. They are gathered around, Jim, Trafford, Celia and Mrs. Kinnell, Cedes clinging to me, blanky in hand, because once again I've caught her just after naptime. It takes a moment for the laptop to boot up. Like most of my residential customers they don't work much with computers, so there's a fascination with the machine quite apart from the plans I've drawn up. There's an authority to it, a sense of magic. It's been great for business.

"Just remember we can change many of the variables," I say, shifting Cedes and sitting down to enter the programme. Heads peer over my shoulder. "I'll get out of the way in a minute," I say. "You really have to look straight on this screen, or things turn a little silver."

The first representation comes up and I let Celia have a look since she's the one paying for all this. "I'll show you the cadillac version first," I say. "I know it's not exactly what you asked for, but we'll aim high and see where we go from there."

"Whose house is that?" Celia asks, adjusting her glasses.

"Well, this house," I say. "One version of it, anyway. This plan would build on the shell of what's already here. What I've programmed the computer to do is expand the upstairs over the garage, as we talked about, but to make it fit in organically with the rest of the house."

"You've put on a kind of new outside, is that right?" Jim says.

"Yes, in a sense. This design would raise the whole roof

three feet, and give you use of the full room space throughout the upper floor."

"Instead of bumping our heads on the slant," Trafford says.

"Exactly," I say. "It's meant for tall people."

"But why do you have to change the outside?" Mrs. Kinnell asks.

"For one thing, the extra structure would require extra
support beams. I also thought this new siding would go well
with the rest of the neighbourhood."

"But it wouldn't be the same house," she says.

"What's wrong with something new?" Trafford says, bending over Celia's shoulder to get a better look. I rotate the image.

"What's that?" Celia asks.

"The view from the backyard," I say, and then when Trafford asks I explain about how the image scanner in the office
converts photos of the property into data which I can then
use for my simulation programme.

"I added a second floor veranda in the back, just as an
option," I say. I go to the inside shots, have the programme
scan room by room.

"My hairdresser has one of these," Celia says. "For $50
you can have the screen show you a picture of what you'll
look like with a certain style before you even have it."

"Well, this is the same sort of idea," I say. I take some papers out of my briefcase. "These are the figures for this
particular renovation. I know it's a lot, but I just wanted to
show you what was possible. Now, if we don't raise the roof,
and if we keep the outside of the house the same as it is now,
as much as possible . . . "

The presentation takes half an hour. I show them four
different versions, which is three too many, but that's the way
I work. They don't decide, of course, but I leave copies of the

estimates with them and promise to do colour printouts for the various options.

Like most people they're a bit glazed with it all, although by the end Trafford has mastered the computer and is switching from picture to picture to compare possibilities. Cedes slowly comes out of her post-nap stupor and begins to squirm. Jim and I take her for a walk to the local park where we swing and make wishes on the snow clouds looming on the edge of the afternoon.

"I remember my Dad came here with me once," Jim says, swinging higher and higher while Cedes and I watch. "He was a very strong man. He kept pumping his legs harder and harder," he says, the swing gathering momentum. He rises to the height of the bar. "Finally," he says, "he went all the way."

"Jim!"

"Go! Go! Higher!" Cedes yells.

"Jim! Stop it!"

He goes so high the chain starts to slacken at the end of the pendulum, and his seat turns a little so that he's looking straight down.

"Jim!"

"What?"

"*Stop!*"

He slows, reluctantly, dragging his feet in the dirt.

"Don't you ever do that when I'm around!"

He smiles, gives me his little boy look.

"I wanted him to go all the way around!" Cedes says.

"Yeah, and break his head!" I say.

"He wouldn't," she says.

"I wouldn't," he says.

"How many children are there here anyway?" I ask.

"Just me," Cedes says. "I'm the only one."

"That's right. Just one," I say, getting up, ready to go. As we walk back, Jim and I each holding one of Cedes's hands, she asks, "Where's my Mommy?"

"I told you that before," Jim says.

"But where's my Mommy?"

"She's in India."

"When is she coming to get me?"

"Christmas."

"And where am I going after that?"

"I don't know."

"I don't want to go."

"Well you'll be happy to see your Mommy."

"Yes," she says in a matter-of-fact voice, and then she stoops to look at something on the road by her feet, a bottle cap.

"I think Mommy should come to stay here," she says when she gets up.

"I think I need a drink," I say as we pull up, the headlights from my Volvo carving beams through the falling snow. Have I paid Mr. Connors for snow removal this year, I wonder, thinking of the farmer on the next property who has a tractor and not a lot to do in the winter. These things to arrange, year after year.

"It's beautiful," Jim says as we get out of the car. He stands in the silver of the new snow looking at my farmhouse. I hope the pipes aren't frozen. It's a little early in the season for that. But not for the lock to be frozen. I can barely get the key in. I hate locks. Jim walks around, his shoes making enormous prints in the wet snow. "It's jammed," I tell him. He opens it, laughing. I blunder through the door and turn on lights, flick on the thermostat, hoping there's oil in the furnace. I can't remember if I called for that. But something rumbles downstairs, so heat should be on its way. Jim gets the bags.

"It's magnificent," he says, coming through the doorway into the kitchen with the sloping floors and the peeling linoleum. "Is there a fireplace?"

I tell him and soon he's out gathering firewood, something else I'll have to order, although there's a remnant pile from last year. I bring in the groceries from the trunk. Jim gets the fire going. I pour myself a glass of wine. Everything's going to be all right, I tell myself. I just wish I'd warm up.

Jim pushes me in front of him a few feet from the fire, blazing now on the euphoria of old newspapers and kindling. My hands warm superficially, but the shivering won't stop. I feel his body behind me. He starts to squeeze my shoulders, push his thumbs down my spine.

"Too hard?" he says as I pull away.

"It's, uh, I just need to warm up," I say.

He starts again and again I pull away. I can't help it. I'm like a cinder block left out in the snow.

"You warm up. I'll make us an omelette," he says.

"Oh, God, I'm not hungry."

"You need food to warm you up. It's basic fuel. This house will be cold for a while."

"I think I'm all right," I say, but he goes into the kitchen anyway. Humming something, not angry. The fire calms down quickly, turns to consume the larger logs that Jim has put on. Over the sighs and the crackles I hear him rattling pots in the kitchen, opening cupboards, cracking eggs. He's singing something. The fragments of what seems like an old song drift in, in a voice that's not his, but deeper, like Trafford might sing, I think:

> *And each night I walk the bend*
> *Till my love is home again,*

Am I singing to the wind?
Or will your heart come back to me?

It's a gentle voice that goes well with kitchen sounds and
the fire. Some of the shaking stops, but I still feel strange inside, a hollowness.

We eat by the fire and talk about the renovations. He's
right, the food warms me, goes well with the wine. I settle
back against him, his arms around me. He slowly works his
fingers through my hair. I think about what to say and he
starts to kiss the back of my neck and I freeze.

"I'm sorry," I say.

"It's all right," he whispers, his hands still moving
through my hair. My face feels hot from the fire but I'm so
cold inside.

"Maybe this isn't a good idea," I say.

"It's nice to just sit here."

"Yes."

And so we do, on and on, his fingers not stopping, but
not knowing what to do either. I don't know what I want them
to do.

He says, "I'll sleep in the spare bedroom."

"No," I say. "The bed is pretty bad. I'll sleep there. You
take my bed."

He thinks about it. His fingers don't stop.

"I can sleep on a lumpy bed," he says. "Probably better
than you."

"How would you know?"

"Are you a good sleeper?"

"Sometimes. Yes."

"I wouldn't have thought so."

"What's that supposed to mean?"

"I always pictured you as sort of a feline sleeper, you know. One slight sound and you're awake."

"Well, if there's noise."

He kisses my neck again. Just like that. One moment he's talking about sleeping in the guest room, and the next his hand is running down my side.

"Jim," I say, moving away.

"Mmmm?"

"Jim!"

"It's okay," he says, kissing my hair.

"What's okay?"

"We don't have to do anything."

"That's fine with me."

"Just because you've brought me here, at night, to this secluded farmhouse."

He kisses my neck again.

"This isn't funny!" I say. He smiles, his eyes glinting with reflected fire.

"No, it's not," he says, giggling.

"No it isn't!"

"Absolutely. It's completely serious. There is no humour in this situation at all." He starts tickling my legs and I scramble off, yelping, spilling my wine all over.

"Now that's very serious!" he says, licking the wine from my hand.

"I thought you didn't like wine."

"Oh, it's terrible stuff!" he says, licking some more. "It makes you do impetuous things. Very silly things you regret later. We should stop right now."

"Yes."

He doesn't stop. I pour some more wine, for him and for me. We don't drink very much of it. He insists on kissing my neck, making me laugh. He seems to like his wine mostly spilled. Oh well, the clothes can be washed. The fire gets low and he says he'll go outside for more wood but doesn't.

"I'm really tired," I say, yawning, laughing.

"Yes, I can tell."

"We should go to bed."

"Yes."

"I'll take the lumpy bed," he says.

"You don't have to."

"Okay. I'll take your bed."

"That's fine."

We start to get up. He takes my hand and brushes against my breast, just like that, almost spilling more wine.

"I feel I owe you an explanation," I say.

He kisses me. We stand, rocking together, kissing, for quite a while. I don't know what to do with the glass I'm holding.

When he lets me I catch my breath and put it down on the floor.

"This isn't familiar territory for me. I think you appreciate that. This isn't something I do every day."

We kiss again, backing against the doorframe leading to the upstairs. I can't seem to get my thoughts together.

"Sometimes," he says, "it's best not to talk."

"But I want to think this through."

"Sometimes . . ." we kiss again, "you really shouldn't think."

"I —"

We start going up the stairs, pausing on each one for breath and a word or two before kissing again.

The top of the stairs. Somehow.

"This is your room. I mean my room."

"Wonderful!" he says and then scoops me up. It's not a rehearsed movement and he almost crashes my head against the doorframe.

"I'm going to sleep in the other —"

"Yes of course," he says, laying me on the bed, cold and sunk in shadows.

"If you think you're seducing me —"

"Absolutely not," he says, taking off my shoes, rubbing my feet and toes through the socks.

"I'm afraid, Jim."

"Yes," he says, stopping, smiling.

"I haven't really decided."

"Of course." He reaches up and unsnaps my jeans, and then pulls them off. I let him. He touches my thigh with the tips of his fingers and spreads goose pimples down the rest of my legs.

"It's cold in here."

"Yes." He takes a folded blanket from the foot of my bed and drapes it over the lower part of my legs. Then he runs his fingers lightly down the insides of my thighs.

"We aren't going to do anything," he says, his head lowered. "I'm going to tickle you for awhile, and then I'm going to go down the hall where I assume my bed is. Okay?"

I nod. His hand runs along the edge of my underwear.

"You haven't asked me what I'm afraid of," I say.

"No," he says.

"It's just . . . I've never . . . I haven't . . . "

He kisses me again, stretches the elastic of my underwear then slips his hand under.

I snap upright, slapping his hand away. "You're not listening to me. You nod, you say 'yes,' and you go right ahead doing exactly what you want."

"Is that a — are you having your . . . ?"

"It's a tampon. I'm having my period. Yes," I say.

His expression freezes — zap! — like I've stunned him in a science fiction movie. The moment is priceless. I start to laugh and he still can't snap out of it.

"What?" he says. "What's so funny?"

"You!"

"Well thanks. Thanks a lot!"

I keep laughing, draw my knee to my chest, then rumple his hair with my foot.

"I'm sorry," I say.

"I don't think you are."

"Well, no, but I thought I'd say it anyway."

He gets up, adjusts his pants where they've gotten tight.

"You could have told me," he says.

"I just did."

"Yes," he says.

"So my room is down here?" he asks, taking a few steps to the door.

I let him reach the hall.

"No," I say. "You're room is in here."

He comes back reluctantly.

"I want to see you with your clothes off," I say.

"What?"

"You took my pants off. Now I want you to take your clothes off. I'll watch." I sit up, bouncing a little, squeaking the springs.

He hesitates, can't quite see my smile in the shadows. Then he takes off his sweater and his shirt in one tugging movement.

He starts to unzip his pants, pulls them down slightly, then remembers and bends to take off his shoes. Then he pulls down his pants.

"Come on, your underwear, let's go!" I say.

He does it.

"Come here. It's cold!" I say, lifting the blanket for him. He slides beside me, is erect on the first touch of my hands.

"Now this is what you were thinking of, isn't it?"

His banter is not so lively now.

I run my fingers up and down his chest. He starts to lift my shirt but I take his hands away. He starts rocking slowly against me.

"Do you mind if I tell you something?" I say.

He opens his eyes, doesn't quite seem capable of conversation.

"I want to do it anyway."

"What?"

"You don't mind, do you?"

Now it's his turn to smile.

"It's the last day probably. There won't be much blood."

"All right." He's still uncertain.

"Do you have AIDS?" I ask. "Did you bring protection?"

"No," he says. "Yes." He stops rocking. "I don't have AIDS. I brought condoms."

"I've never asked anyone before," I say.

"Whether they have AIDS or whether they brought protection?"

"Whether they want to do it. I mean, *I've* never asked. I never thought I would."

"Garland," he says.

"Yes?"

"You're really kooky sometimes."

"I know. It's your fault. Do you mind?"

"No," he says.

TWENTY-TWO

It passes swiftly. I hold on like I'm in a tropical storm and there isn't time to know what to do, to figure out these feelings. Is this what all the fuss is about? Then I haven't been missing so much. As I knew already. It's almost a relief. Jim is snoring on his back in minutes. He takes the storm with him, leaving me gasping and utterly awake. Sixty watts of light creeps in from the hallway to scratch the corners of my eyes. Who is this boy? Why him? Why now?

I suppose I should feel grateful. Deflowered finally by someone who sleeps this deeply, by a long-boned boy with tiny hairs around his nipples and a flush on his cheeks and muscles, corded, springy, young male muscles. How Daddy would love to see this moment. Ha! Finally brought down to earth! Finally you know. You're just like the rest of us.

Jim turns over, snuggles into the pillow. I adjust the blankets, feel like it's seven o'clock in the morning and the first jolt of coffee has hit home. How can I sleep now? This wasn't enough. It was only a taste, a start. I was just feeling warm. I know there is more. He throws his arm over me, his eyes still closed. Those enormous hands. There Daddy, look, his hands are beautifully kept. He should know how to touch a woman. We'll have to do it again, that's all. Bring it on again, more slowly this time. That one was for him.

This is how it gets you. You stay strong for so many years. Then someone comes along and you have to take the ride with him because there's no other contentment now, and once you've done it you have to do it again, it's over so fast and leaves you so dizzy you can't grasp it. These things I know before I've done them. I knew it wouldn't be enough. It would be the start, a yearning, a hunger, a need that wasn't there before. I was fine. I ran my own business, made my own meals, talked to myself. Now I'm lying awake at night with my body tingling and sweaty, my tissues aching and yearning in ways they never have before.

He snuggles against me, eyes still closed. It's an intimate thing to see someone sleep, almost more so than to share bodies in a collision of lovemaking. I put my hand against his cheek, check the digital clock glowing in the corner. Two thirty-seven. It could be hours before I'm asleep. I slip out of bed, pull on my socks and nightie, snuggle in beside him again. I'm used to having more room. It feels strange.

I was safe where I was, I think. I thought I was happy. Now everything is different.

More snow in the morning. Is it going to be one of those winters? I wake up with my eyelids feeling like they've been stretched too tight against my eyes. It's only when I swing out of bed that I realize he's not here. His clothes are on the floor, his pants and underwear squatting on his shoes with no actual body left. I glance out the window and see my car still there, huddled in snow. But there are footprints beside it, the strides enormous.

I'm in the bath when he returns. As he bursts into the bathroom I think of a horse — the sweaty muscles, the flecks of foam, the good-natured, breathy noises. The smell of strain and effort, the pure body size. He peels down to skin, another pile of clothes squatting on the floor, and slips into the bath beside me, the cold air still wrapped around him.

"How far did you go?" I ask, trying not to stare. His penis

is shrivelled and old-looking, like some troll hiding under a bridge.

"It's the cold," he says, laughing. "Don't worry, it'll recover. How are you?" And then he leans over and kisses me, like this is it, the one place in the world where he wants to be.

"I haven't told you how beautiful you are," he says. "You've probably heard it too much anyway. But you are utterly beautiful." He starts to soap my legs, my tummy, gently touches my breasts. He says, "I woke up this morning with a nuclear reactor inside me. I just had to get up. I went along that dirt road out back. I didn't know how far it would go, and I had to be careful of my footing. But there are some mornings you feel like your legs have springs in them."

He gives me the soap and I wash his legs which indeed feel like they have springs in them. They are long and tapered and strong. Then I soap his torso, his middle, his storm of pubic hair. He does get bigger, very quickly. It's an extraordinary thing to be sharing a bath with a young man who has come in from a run, and sweats like a horse, and has such appendages, and looks at me with such eyes.

It takes a long time to make it down to breakfast. First we have to dry off, and go back to the bedroom, and get back in bed. Slower, slower this time I think but I don't need to tell him. He already knows. He touches me and kisses me until I'm warm, until I'm boiling from the inside, such a strange feeling, like there are valves here I didn't know about, juices I didn't think I had. Slowly, slowly. This time it's for me. It's light, we can see each other, the room is finally warm. I touch all his body, kiss the gentle skin behind his knee, between his thighs, along the gnarled trunk of his penis. How medieval it looks.

There's no talking this time. It's much gentler, like we're trying to fill the glass beyond the brim but not overflow. How do I know we're trying to do this? It stays at the brim for a long time, and then there is the falling, the sweetness inside, that happens unexpectedly, stops me in my motion, makes me gasp and cling to him. Something new. I had no idea. I didn't know this would happen. He starts to smile even as I feel the pulse inside me, and when I get my breath back we both start to giggle, two children discovering a secret room.

"This is my grandfather's favourite meal," he says, when we're finally downstairs sitting at the kitchen table.

"I didn't even know I had oatmeal," I say.

"Well, I wasn't sure, so I brought some," he says.

"In your luggage?"

"It's a very good fuel," he says, glopping some in a bowl for me.

"Did you bring brown sugar?"

"I brought some for you, yes," he says, producing a small jar.

"You won't have some?"

"Well, I've learned to eat it like my grandfather does. Just straight with a large glass of warm water. It does wonders for the digestive system."

He spoons down enormous amounts from one of my cooking bowls.

"If I hang around you I'm going to have to keep up my strength," he says.

In the afternoon we walk in the backwoods along my favourite trail. I wear my floppy black rubber boots and an enormous old sweater of Dad's. I show him my stream, and we cross the stepping stones holding hands so that when he slips he almost brings me down with him except I let go and he balances on one leg, waving his arms like a clown before he recovers. Then we stand in the middle laughing at how he almost slipped and how I let him go.

"Is that the way it's going to be?" he says. "Should I be worried?"

We walk further into the woods, where the light is silvery and the air still. It's my place. I've not brought anyone here before. But it's like he has been here all along, belongs here as much as I do. A blue jay leaves a branch up ahead and snow falls onto the trail ahead of us. We step over a dead tree that has been rotting as long as I've been coming here, blown over in some storm years ago.

Jim stops to listen to something and I turn toward him because for a moment I've forgotten the exact look of his eyes. He starts laughing and so do I, and then I ask him what he's laughing about.

"I don't know," he says, and laughs again.

TWENTY-THREE

"Something's different," Roxanne says when she sees me. Well, her hair for one; she has had it cut close to the scalp like a teenager's. And the fact that we're having lunch again only two months from our last one and that I'm the one on time. She sits down in a bustle of curiosity.

"It's very interesting," I say, looking at her hair.

"Oh the do," she says dismissively. "I got it cut because of the shelter. Where I'm working. To fit in better. A lot of the girls have done it."

"You're working?"

"Volunteer work. Three mornings. Well, it's a way to escape the kids anyway." So we talk about her new work, and the kids, and Robert's conferences — he goes to a lot of conferences — but before the meal has arrived she's back to her original observation.

"There's something different," she says. "Something has happened."

"Well," I say, embarrassed, and she claps her hands and shrieks so that everyone else in the restaurant looks at us.

"It's a man! I knew it! I knew it as soon as I saw you. It's a man!" she announces.

"Roxanne!" I say, shushing her.

"I'm sorry! I'm sorry!" she whispers, "I'm sorry!"

"It's all right."

"I took one look at you and I thought — "

The waiter appears, a saviour, asking if we'd like anything to drink.

"Yes!" Roxanne says immediately. "Champagne!" and when we laugh I feel like the schoolgirl I never was, giddy over something shared and so achingly funny it makes the world jiggly as Jell-O.

"You'll have to start at the beginning," Roxanne says.

I try. Heaven knows I have heard all about Robert hanging around under Roxanne's window in university, how they went to France together and split up four times in eight days, how he flew home to be with someone else and she stayed to pick grapes and when she got back, having told no one her itinerary, there he was at the airport with flowers. It occurs to me that these things are a bit rushed and confused when they happen and then over time become infused with the inevitability of legend. Things might have worked out between Robert and the other girl. Theirs might have been the story infused with inevitability.

Part of this sort of thinking keeps me from explaining too much. But also it's very new, what's happening. I don't want to share it so much. So I'm a disappointing lunch partner, even more so than before, when I didn't have such interesting news. I start to apologize, try to explain.

"Hey, listen," she says. "Don't worry about it. I know how you're feeling. You'll bring him to dinner on Saturday, all right?"

I tell her I really think we should give it some more time.

"I hear, I understand completely," she says. "Absolutely. You're in love, you just want to go away and feel it. I know. We'll do dinner another time."

"Thanks."

"How about Sunday?"

"Roxanne!"

"Just kidding!"

But it's like that. Just wanting him for myself. I get through the day telling myself I won't phone. Today is for me. I'll have a quiet evening and deal with that backlog of work and then fall asleep early. I promise myself. But I call him anyway, just to feel the warmth when he knows it's me. We talk about nothing, really, things that have happened to the computers, a house I'm working on, something funny one of the nurses said in class. We both say how tired we are, how nice it'll be to get a good night's sleep.

"What are you doing for dinner?" he asks.

"Nothing. Just fixing something here."

"I was going to go for a run. Maybe I could head out in your direction."

"Okay. But I really want an early night tonight."

"Absolutely. I'm just beat. I could fall asleep right now."

Afterwards, lying in bed with the air sweet like it has finally rained. That delicious feeling of just being still. "Tomorrow, little girl," he says in some phoney accent, the glow of my digital clock on his forehead, "you're going to bed early, and we're both going to get some sleep."

I have dinner with his family. They haven't decided yet which renovation plan to follow. The subject seems to be a bit of an embarrassment and I don't pursue it past the opening cocktail which Mrs. Kinnell pours with relish. "Finally, somebody in the family who drinks!" she says, bringing me a rye and ginger. She knows that her son and I have become lovers, tells me with her first glance that she's happy, makes me feel comfortable entering her home on this new footing.

Cedes has lined up all her shoes in the living room and has put tiny dolls to bed in them, so we're forced to whisper so they won't wake up. She climbs on my lap and starts to play with my hair.

"Do you think my Mommy has long hair?" she whispers.

"I wouldn't know. Don't you remember?"

"Sometimes she has long hair, but sometimes she doesn't." She tells me again that her Mommy is coming to get her at Christmas.

"We're going to go on an airplane after that," she says, "but we have to be careful not to scare Santa Claus."

"I don't think you will," I say. "Where are you going on the airplane?"

"To Farland," she says, nodding her head solemnly. Then, changing tones, "Celia is going on an airplane."

"Oh?" I say, raising my eyebrows and turning to Trafford

who's having a large glass of buttermilk. "Is Celia going on an airplane?"

"Her mother is sick," he says briefly. "She's going to Aberdeen."

"Shhhh!" Cedes says, pointing to her dolls.

Later, when I'm helping Mrs. Kinnell chop the vegetables, she tells me that Celia's mother is ninety-eight and has lived on her own till just this week when she broke her hip climbing the attic stairs to get the storm windows.

"How long will Celia be gone?" I ask.

"Now that's the question," she says.

It's a tense meal, focused mostly on getting Cedes to eat her peas and potatoes which she spreads around with her fork and then pouts over. Mrs. Kinnell coaxes her with promises of dessert. Trafford yells at her that there'll be no further food till the vegetables are downed. Jim rescues her juice three times from spilling. Finally the little girl flees in tears.

"She needs discipline," Trafford says angrily. "Her mother had no discipline, and now she has no discipline."

"Every child goes through a difficult eating phase," Mrs. Kinnell says.

"And there's only one way to handle it," Trafford says, grimly downing his own vegetables. "Spare the rod . . . "

"I'm very sorry my dear," Mrs. Kinnell says, touching my arm with her hand.

"We should never have accepted to look after the child," Trafford says.

"I don't believe that *we* did," Mrs. Kinnell says. "I think *I* was the one who accepted."

"Imagine a woman leaving her child with someone else to raise. Abandon a child. Imagine!"

"She has hardly abandoned her child. She'll be back at Christmas."

"Christmas what year?" Trafford says. "Knowing Mirele, she mightn't return till the child is eighteen. Did you ever think of that?"

"I don't recall you raising these objections when Mirele was here," Mrs. Kinnell says.

Jim asks his grandfather to pass the potatoes, and we eat in silence, except for Cedes's crying upstairs. Finally I excuse myself and pick up her plate.

"She won't have a bite of it," Trafford says as I get up. "She's completely spoiled and wilful."

"That's all right," I say. "So was I."

I approach her room quietly, gently knock on the door.

"Go away!" she screams.

"Cedes, it's Garland. Can I come in?"

There's a long silence, and so I go in. The room is mostly dark with a small light on in the corner, by the bed. The shadows make me think suddenly of my own room so many years ago.

"I don't want that!" she yells, pointing in agony at the plate.

"It's okay, you don't have to eat anything." I put the plate on her dresser and sit on the edge of the bed. "I think I need a hug," I say, stroking her hair. "You know, my Mommy died when I was just born. I never knew her in my whole life. I know what it is to be lonely."

She doesn't say anything.

"There are going to be times when it feels like you're all that you've got, there's no one else. So you have to be, you'll have to be strong inside. Do you know what I mean, strong inside?"

She nods her head infinitesimally.

"You'll feel like you're all alone. In fact it's never true. There's always somebody else. You won't always know it. You won't always let them in. But they're there."

She crawls around so that she's sitting on my lap and lays her head against my arm.

"I used to cry a lot too," I say. "My father raised me by himself. I thought it was so unfair, that I was so unlucky. I never thought he might be lonely too, that he might think it was unfair. I always took it for granted that he'd be there, and that it wouldn't be enough. Anyway, I'm sure this isn't helping at all. Just remember that your mother loves you, and that whatever happens, you have a family right here."

"Garland?"

"Yes, sweetie?"

"I don't want to eat my peas, okay?"

"Okay."

We agree on cheese flakes and toast, a heresy in Trafford's eyes, but Mrs. Kinnell overrides him. At the table we settle into a silence that reminds me of sitting with Daddy when he really only wanted to read the newspaper but didn't because it was "bad manners," and so we watched each other chew. Is this what everyone's family life is like?

And then, in a sudden gust of winter wind, she's there at the door, as if conjured by our earlier discussion.

"Good God!" Trafford says when the drapes blow back. Mirele appears in the doorway shouldering an enormous knapsack: wild black hair, skin deep brown; hiking boots and bluejeans; a flash of white smile that seems to draw the poor light of the hallway and magnify it.

Trafford's fork bounces off the corner of his plate and clatters to the floor. Jim turns to look but remains sitting. Cedes glances at the intruder and then looks back at her plate, apparently unaware of who has arrived. Only Mrs. Kinnell gets up to greet her.

"I should've phoned," Mirele says as Mrs. Kinnell closes the door against the winter. "But I thought it would be a surprise. Hello, Trafford!" she calls, and Trafford lumbers to his feet. She tosses her hair and the movement for a moment reminds me of Darlene.

"It has been so long since I've seen *you!*" she says to Jim, and when he stands up she hugs him like the long-lost lovers they are.

"Are you taller than you were?" she says, and before he can answer, "I hear you're a professor now. Are you still writing?"

My quizzical glance catches his eye.

"Well, uh," he says and she interrupts him again.

"James used to read me poetry constantly. He was always quoting Shakespeare and Donne. And some of his own poems too."

"Lots of people write poetry when they're teenagers," he says. Mirele turns her attention to Cedes.

"*You* have grown *enormous!* I don't believe you. Here, give me a hug!"

Cedes turns obediently, her eyes still on her cheese flakes, as if that's what she's really interested in. Mirele hoists her up and carries her part-way into the living room. Cedes plays with her mother's hair and discovers a pair of feathered earrings.

"I have a feather too!" she says, and scrambles down to run to the other room to find it. She returns in a moment brandishing a gull's feather. "This is a wing that Grandpa gave me!"

"God, I missed you," Mirele says, poking Cedes through a hole in her dress where her belly is pulling the buttons apart. "Did you miss me? Huh? Did you miss me?"

Cedes says, "The birds flew right up, and then they flew right up and *whooshed* us into the air . . ." (her hands whooshing with the feather) "and you know where we went?"

"Where?" Mirele asks.

"We went to Farland to visit my mother!"

I'm introduced simply as "Garland." The name sticks for a moment against the roof of Jim's mouth and his eyebrows furrow in the effort to remember me. It only takes a few minutes for the blood to stop moving in my body, for air to leave the room.

"No, really, I can't stay, it's been lovely, thank you," I say to Mrs. Kinnell at the door, jamming my feet into my boots. Jim is still in the dining room.

"Where are you going?" Cedes asks, waving her feather at me.

"Oh, I have some work to do, honey," I say, and Jim looks up as if there's something vaguely familiar about my voice.

And then there's cold air, and I walk to my car, doing up my coat, trying not to slip on the ice. I can't get the fucking key in the lock. I'm there long enough, swearing, trying to steady my hand. He could come out to talk to me. But he doesn't, and I get the door open, and then I leave.

TWENTY-FOUR

"You don't have any money," Daddy says to me from the doorway. I have my back to him. His shadow reaches into the room. I'm almost finished putting everything I need — mostly my books — into my one big suitcase. I don't know if I'll be able to carry it.

"Just put that stuff away. You don't have any money. You're going off half-cocked."

I tug at the zipper, kneeling on the suitcase to get it closed. I wish I didn't feel so goddamn weak.

"I'm your father! I have a right to know where you think you're going! Talk to me! Do you hear?"

"Yes, I can hear you," I say in my severest whisper. He still hasn't come into the room. He's still just a shadow.

"What's the problem? Let's talk it over. You're the most stubborn — "

"*I don't want to be in anybody's way!*" I scream, pulling up the suitcase with both hands. "*I'm eighteen years old! I can look after myself! I don't need anybody! Okay?*"

He gives me his look like I'm a golf ball that won't fall into the cup. But he's just a shadow, he won't stop me.

I drag the suitcase down the stairs. I'm right. He's just a shadow. He doesn't say a word.

It's the same now. I drive through the blackened streets, the world outside shifting in murk. I check my messages on my car phone, and for the first time I can remember there's nothing there, not even a plea for money. I don't know where to go. My safe place, the farmhouse, has been invaded — it's where we made love. His spoor is in my condo, too, which seems empty, too much my office. Work is there. The thought of it makes me want to vomit.

I dial Roxanne's number and put the phone down when Robert answers. What am I thinking of? I couldn't just crash there. There would be explanations to make, social obligations, conversation. She'd want to know every fucking detail. She'd say something like, "Let's look at the bright side." There is no bright side. I've waited till age thirty-five to become a total idiot, and now I'm getting what I deserve.

The look on his face. Exactly what I deserve. For thinking

I could escape, like getting out of chicken pox as a child and then coming down with them years later, those ridiculous red spots, itching and blistered.

I drive some more. I stop in the parking lot of the Maple Lounge Motel and watch three couples go into the main reception cabin. One couple obviously married, tired from a long trip, not talking. Another obviously having an affair; his eyes nervous, scanning the area for spies; her breathing too fast, her clothes too skimpy for this weather.

The third couple is elderly and slow. They hold hands to manage the traverse across the ice. He gets the door for her, then later goes back for the luggage. I can picture them in pyjamas: they have grown children, grandchildren they talk to on the phone. He holds her when he goes to sleep and snores in her ear and she doesn't mind, is deaf anyway.

I go back to my condo. There's a message. The red light on my answering machine jump-starts my nervous system as soon as I open the door. But it isn't from Jim. It's a voice from the Earth Committee, asking for funds, leaving a number.

There's no sleep. Eyelids scratch across eyeballs in the darkness and little voices go through every possible time I could have refused him, should have done it, could have avoided this catastrophe. I was strong, independent, happy. Neurotic, yes, but I could live with that. I was working on it. I was doing all right. Now this.

Dawn comes as a relief, an excuse to stop trying to sleep. I do my best day's work in a month, not stopping for lunch, my mind whirring like a little motor that goes and goes and goes. I order in for dinner, keep working till after midnight, turn out the lights, and still the motor whirrs.

All night again. Conversations repeating themselves. "I didn't want this," I say to him again and again, my finger poking his chest. "You made me get involved with you but I didn't want this. Do you understand that? This wasn't a game to me. I wasn't looking for something to tide me over till my true love came back. I'm stronger than that. I don't need you. You've just wasted a great deal of my time and energy. Don't call me again, all right? Am I clear? Do you understand?"

(But he doesn't call. This brilliant speech runs over and over in my head like one of those cable TV movies. I could let him have it at any moment. But he doesn't call.)

The next day I collapse at the computer, am out for only fifteen minutes but can't think after that. I get Janice to hold my calls. I retreat to my bedroom, can't sleep. It's so unfair. I didn't ask for this.

Roxanne calls in the evening, asking me to bring Jim to her Christmas party. I listen to her voice on the answering machine, try to think of what to say. I don't call back.

Somehow I've known all my life it was going to be this way if I ever fell in love. Some people aren't meant to have love work out, and I'm one of them. I'll draw you a gable, build you a bathroom, design your indoor pool so that it lasts a hundred years. But I'm the girl who never had a mother. I can't dance to save my life. I'm not meant for love. It fits me badly.

I look in the mirror, for the first time in months really examine my face. Tired, yes, pale — my winter look. And there it is between my eyes, a new wrinkle to go with the frown lines. I pull at my eyebrows and it vanishes, then reappears as soon as I let go.

The artisans who worked on the Taj Mahal were put to death after its completion so that no building more beautiful would ever be built. Maybe that's the way to go, to leave something perfect and heavenly behind. Most of life is too messy for me anyway — I like straight lines, clean curves, the clear morning light arching through a span of windows.

Someone rings the buzzer from downstairs but I don't answer it, leafing through a coffee table book of architecture in Florence that my father gave me. I've never been to Florence. Maybe it's what I need to do. Pack up my sketchpad. Sell the farmhouse — no, the office if anything. Shut it right down.

The door bell rings this time. It's probably one of my clients. Someone probably let him in through the security doors. It's only when I get up that it occurs to me that it could be Jim. Crawling back for forgiveness. Clutching flowers. Forget it. I don't want to be second choice. I won the Doleman Award for Excellence in Architecture. There was no second prize. Second place doesn't count.

I look through the view hole just to see him and what kind of flowers he has. But it isn't him, it's his mother, ringing and knocking and calling my name.

"Oh dear," she says, stepping back when I finally open the door. "I hope I didn't get you from something."

"I was hoping I'd find you in," she says. "I tried calling but all I got was your machine." She blows a bit of grey hair out of her eyes. "Well, I thought I should tell you that Trafford and Celia have gone to Scotland. So I'm afraid we aren't going to do our renovations after all. I'm very disappointed as I'm sure you are too. Please bill us for your time so far. I'd like you to talk to James. He's being a complete idiot. He hasn't called, has he?"

I shake my head.

"I was afraid of that. Like a lot of men he, well, he gets muddled," she says. "I should never have agreed to take in Mercedes."

She looks down a moment at the snow dripping off her boots.

"Will you come with me to lunch?" she asks finally. "We have some talking to do. And you look like you could use some food."

We go in her car, not to a restaurant as I imagined but to a small apartment on the other end of town, a sprawling end unit from the 1930s that has been added onto four or five times. The entrance is from the back, up an iron firescape slippery from the snow.

"Everybody needs a place they can go," she says, unlocking the door and then banging her boots on the mat. "A refuge of sorts. Just completely away."

It's a tiny apartment with a four-poster bed, a soft rug, a kitchenette in the corner, and the smallest bathroom I've ever seen. There's a batik on the wall over the bed quite different from anything in her house — oriental blues swirling, a woman with two lovers.

"Take off your boots, dear," she says. "I'll put the soup on."

We sit on the carpet by the window eating mushroom soup from a can. It warms everything, just like the commercial says it will.

"I wasn't sure if this was the right thing to do," she says. "Bringing you here." She doesn't look in my eyes but at my socks instead, as if choosing her words from among the loose threads. "One thing I've found is that there are times in life when it seems like you have options, a difficult choice to make. One thing or the other. This road or that. You worry and wonder and then, when you get close to it all, usually the choice just disappears. It was an illusion. There wasn't *really* a choice."

I finish my soup. I don't know what her point is.

"The heart knows," she says, looking up. "Sometimes

things don't work out the way you think they will, but the heart knows. And James has a good heart."

We don't get much past that. There's a rumble on the fire escape and the door opens. At first I think it's Jim, that this has all been set up by Mrs. Kinnell to get us together. But it isn't. A burly, nearly bald man comes through the door, shedding winter clothing, carrying a bottle of wine and a single, shivering red rose.

"Company!" he says with some alarm when he sees me.

"Lee, I'd like you to meet Garland. The young woman I told you about. Do you remember?"

He evidently doesn't, but makes a gallant attempt to cover up. "Ah yes, you're ah, yes."

"James's friend," says Mrs. Kinnell.

"Of course, yes, I knew that!" he says. I'm struck by the way she smiles at him, mockingly, and he returns as good as he gets, several unspoken conversations happening in an instant in the kitchen they evidently share.

"You're the, uh — "

"Architect," Mrs. Kinnell answers for me.

"Yes, of course. I was hoping to meet you. Without you people wouldn't have much need for me." He smiles when he sees that I don't follow. "Cabinet-maker," he says, and it dawns on me that this is the one Jim's mother had the affair with all those years ago. Clearly this is what she wants to show me. Do I understand? I'm not sure. God, she must be dying to talk about it. Keeping this secret for so long.

I don't stay. I call for a taxi and Mrs. Kinnell walks me to the fire escape.

"Do you keep this place together, then?" I ask. She nods. "And you meet here?"

"Wednesday afternoons." She takes my arm as we go down

the slippery steps. "Lee is divorced now. He wants us to marry. But I won't. Things are fine this way."

"But surely you'd be happier."

"It's Trafford and James," she says. "They really couldn't adjust very well. The whole idea, it was very hard for them. There's a wooden streak in the men in the family. They aren't flexible. This was a better solution."

She's getting cold in the wind. Her lover is waiting for her.

"You are welcome in my family," she says. "Whatever happens. You are welcome."

"Thank you," I say.

TWENTY-FIVE

The weather turns the next day. A deep freeze sits on the city driving ice up the windows, killing car batteries, imprisoning souls like myself who don't ski or skate or enjoy breathing refrigerated air. I'm reminded of Daddy dragging me out on those polar days in snowsuits that did nothing to keep away the cold. Maybe that's why I hate the winter now, swear every year I won't take it any more, will retreat south, design condo space in Florida. Every year the bad weather comes too early, takes me by surprise.

As does Jim's knock at my door. It's two in the morning. I only hear it because I'm lying half-awake wondering when the glaciers will recede and give me back my life. I've seen love now and it's over-rated. I walk to the door, pulling on my robe like a zombie. How did he get past the security doors downstairs? "Hi! Did I wake you?" he says.

I close the door again and head back to bed.

The knocking continues, but this time he rings the bell too. I open the door.

"If I had a gun I'd shoot you," I say. I close the door.

I shut the bedroom door, turn on my stereo and hide under the covers. I can still hear him — fainter, more rhythmic. In for the long haul.

I go back after half an hour. "You're going to wake up everybody in the building!" I say.

"Come for a walk with me?" he says.

"It's Antarctica out there!"

"It's not too bad. Come for a walk with me."

"I don't believe you." I close the door again.

"Please," he says through the wood.

"Go with Mirele. I'm sure she'd enjoy it."

"Mirele's gone."

I hesitate. I shouldn't get into this conversation. I should just go back to bed.

"They've gone back to India."

I start back towards the bedroom.

"She wanted me to come with her. I said no."

"Who wanted you to come?"

There's a pause. "Mercedes," he says.

"What did Mirele want?"

"God knows what Mirele wants. I didn't ask her."

"What did *you* want?"

"You. Come for a walk? Please?"

It's the stupidest thing I should consider, I know. But what else am I supposed to do at two-thirty in the morning, sleep? I put on every stitch of warm clothing I can find. I pull on my boots, long coat, scarf, hat, mitts. It's like I'm eight years old again. So this is more of what love is.

When I open the door he's slumped in the hallway, his back to the wall.

"Thank you," he whispers.

"I'm not going far. This is ridiculous. I don't even know why I'm talking to you."

With the first step outside a gale penetrates my clothing. Jim tries to say something but my hat, collar and scarf make it hard to hear.

"What?" I yell.

"I want to go down to the river!"

"Are you crazy?"

"Yes!"

We go down to the fucking river. It's a fifteen minute walk from here, a necessarily silent passage, in single file along the snow-narrowed sidewalk. I watch his feet ahead of me to not get lost. I could just stop and go back. He probably wouldn't notice. I don't know why I don't except if I made a wrong step I might end up dying of exposure in some snow-bank. Another sad case for the tabloids. When we get to the river he turns to me and yells something else, pointing.

"What?"

"This is where my father's ashes are," he says. He moves down the bank, close to the ice, out of the wind. I stay where I am but he motions to me to follow.

"It's also where my father brought my mother," he says, when I join him, "on a night just like this. There should be a spot."

He puts his foot experimentally onto the ice.

"Jim. Don't!"

"There should be a spot here that doesn't freeze," he

says. He takes a quick stride to a rock. "It should be right over here."

"Jim!"

"It's okay. I know this spot. I'll be all right. There should be . . . "

"Jim! Come on back!"

He steps onto the ice.

"This isn't funny! Get back here! You idiot!"

He presses his weight down, steps forward, presses his weight again.

"Jim!"

"I don't understand," he says.

"Come off of there!"

"There's supposed to be a spot right next to here," he says, his face in shadows, his voice full of disbelief and disappointment.

"Please!" I dart to the rock.

"You don't understand."

"No. I don't. Get the fuck off of there!"

"My father took my mother out, and he pointed to this very spot where I'm standing, and he said, 'That's us, right there, you and me.' Because that was the spot that never froze, no matter how cold it got, the water always ran free."

"I'm leaving!" I yell. "You can fall through if you want. I'm not staying here!" I dart back off the rock, scramble up the bank.

"*Garland!*"

I turn. Can't see him. His form has disappeared. Shit.

Down the bank. Tripping. Face full of snow. I get up. He must have fallen through.

No. He's there in front of me, on the rock. "Are you all right?" he asks.

I step across, push him as hard as I can, watch as he spirals backwards, his full weight crashing on whatever sacred spot this is supposed to be. If it's going to break it'll break. But it holds. I take off as fast as I can.

He catches me a hundred metres up the road.

"Stop! Please! This isn't what I expected."

I stop but don't turn. My face is numb from the wind. He takes my arm but I rip it away. He walks around to face me.

"I'm sorry."

"For what?"

"For everything," he says.

I feel like pushing him again, striking out, just to let him know.

"My father took my mother out on a night like this."

"You don't understand, do you?" I'm screaming, out of control. "This isn't about your father or your mother! This is now. I'm me! *Don't you ever jump on the fucking ice in front of me again! Okay?*"

He stands stunned. I know I told him the story. He's just being a jerk.

"I was going to ask you to marry me," he says.

"No."

His face drops.

"Don't ask me like this. I'm furious with you. Don't ask me like this."

He nods his head, taking instructions.

"You can't just spring things on me. I don't work that way. I don't go from reverse to fifth gear without a lot of intermediary stuff. You know? I need a foundation. I need support beams. The whole package has to be thought out. Don't drag me out in the middle of winter, scare me half to death and then propose. Who do you think I am, anyway?"

He stammers something, muddling in his boots.

"Just shut up. Don't ruin things even more."

"Okay," he says, turning.

"Where are you going?"

"Home?"

"No," I say. "First you have to walk me home. Then you're going to have to make me hot chocolate. I'll still be cold, so you'll have to draw me a hot bath and rub my back."

"Okay."

"If I'm still not sleepy you're going to have to make me feel all cuddly and safe and warm."

"All right."

"You're not forgiven."

"Okay."

"It'll take a very long time for you to be forgiven."

"Yes."

"And whatever happened with Mirele —"

"Yes?"

"I don't want to hear about it."

"All right," he says.

We reach the door of my building.

"What happened with Mirele?" I ask.

"I thought you said you didn't want to know?"

"I changed my mind."

He shuffles his feet, waiting for me to open the door so we can talk where it's warm. I stand my ground. I'm going to melt into mush if I go back inside. I want to hear this with winter in my face.

"She was living in Goa," he says. "She said there were a lot of free spirits there from the sixties, deeply spiritual people. She thought I could really get into my meditation there, that Cedes would broaden herself. She had pictures. There was a very nice beach."

I wait for more. He seems stuck. "Did you sleep with her?" I ask.

He doesn't answer. I almost lose sense of where my feet are.

"Mirele and I were lovers as teenagers," he says. "Somebody like that has a power over you. You've nothing to hide from them. It's, it's the hardest thing to explain."

"That's okay," I say, turning, inserting the key. Of course it gets stuck. "You don't have to make me hot chocolate," I say.

"I didn't sleep with her."

The key won't turn.

"I realized I didn't want to. There was only one person I wanted to be with."

I break it. Right there in the fucking lock, it snaps off in my fingers.

"Please believe me."

The floodgates open. I hate crying in front of men. They don't understand. They don't understand a fucking thing.

"How did you get in the building?" I ask.

"There's a door open around back." He holds me, tighter than I want. It feels better than it should.

"Are you all right?"

"I'm just thinking of that little girl," I say. "What's she going to grow up like? Her Mom dragging her around like that. God, families."

I nearly slip. He holds me up. We head around back, not saying anything.

TWENTY-SIX

After Christmas the weather clears, it gets warm for a spell, rains like crazy, then freezes again, silvering telephone lines, tree branches, railings, steps, sidewalks. In the morning Jim works for twenty minutes hacking the ice from my windshield, then we're off, the highway salted bare as we leave the city behind. The sun rises behind us, lacquers the fields in a wonderland glow that would be too fake for a postcard. A little boy skates on top of the snow, chasing a puck, his hat falling off. A dog skitters in circles trying to catch his tail. Near the airport a plane rumbles low over us, wheels retracting like testicles in the cold.

I laugh — imagine, knowing what testicles look like when they get cold! Jim looks at me — what? — and I laugh again.

These things we know and see in everyday life and never talk about.

It isn't such a long drive. But it's been five years since I've taken it. There's always been an excuse. Work, mostly. That's enough. We've talked on the telephone. Pretty good for where we were. Pretty good for my family.

I have a hard time finding the new address. The turn-off was supposed to be ten kilometres after Blunt Crossing but the first road I take, at ten and three-quarters, is the wrong one and I have to phone from the car. It's the next one, thirteen kilometres. If you're going to bother giving distances...

"It doesn't matter," Jim says. "Not everybody's as exact as you."

Great, he's already taking the other side.

In the end it's impossible to miss. From a kilometre away the wind billows through the domed white tent in the clearing, the surface starched by the ice, sheened somehow like an inflatable foam cookie. Jim asks me if it's for indoor tennis. Silly boy.

Dad comes out in his shirtsleeves. He surprises me, looks smaller than before. Has he lost weight? And he has a tan. My father never has a tan. He looks better than I expected. He hugs me, like the long-lost daughter I am, and I surprise myself by hugging back. I lose it right away, but don't want him to see me cry. It's not supposed to be this way.

"Daddy. Let's go inside. You'll get cold." I let go, turn my face away. "Daddy, this is Jim," I say as we walk towards the side door of the little trailer house beside the monstrosity.

"You know, we never thought she'd ever find anyone to put up with her. You're an amazing man, son," he says, slapping Jim with his bad hand, showing off. "I like you already."

Darlene has been baking: shortbread, fruit cake, gingerbread, spiced rolls, scones. She's thicker than she used to be, has cut her hair, still smiles like she owns the world. In about two minutes she owns Jim, batting her big eyes, pushing food on him. "They aren't so bad," he whispers to me in a private moment as we get up to clear some dishes.

No, they aren't so bad.

"I like him," Darlene says to me in the galley kitchen, switching to straight girl talk. In the other room I can hear Dad asking Jim about his work.

"Where did you meet him?" Darlene asks.

"Just in a class I was taking," I say.

The trailer is tiny, like a ship's cabin, rocking perceptibly whenever someone moves. The walls are full of Darlene's paintings, miniature landscapes, frameless most of them, many watercolours, some oils. Bowls of fruit. Winter scenes. A muddy picture of a woman.

"Well, I have to have something to do," she says. "I certainly can't talk to your father all day." The way she says it reminds me that she knows him at least as well as I do, better probably. Yes, for certain, better.

We walk inside the driving range. An eerie yellow light gives everything a space station quality. A huge fan blows air into the structure but there's no heater; it's just as cold inside as out. Still there are three addicts hard at it, whacking away with the regularity of machines, the balls flying in quick arcs abruptly meeting the net and returning to the phoney green astroturf. Jim starts to explain about the one game he played with Trafford.

"You play?" Dad asks, the interest needle jumping erect in his eyes.

"There was just this one time," he says. "My grandfather took me out to an old pasture course. He thought every young man should be acquainted with the game. He hated it himself, but he was from Scotland, so it was like a birthright, inescapable. I never imagined it could be so hard to hit a stationary ball."

It happens right before my eyes. I'm too late to stop it. Dad has him on the practice mat, drawing the club back, keeping his head down, focusing his fucking inner strength.

"They're gone," Darlene says.

"We shouldn't have come in here."

We leave them, retreat to the warmth of the cabin. Darlene lights a cigarette, the stuffiness filling the room immediately. When did she start smoking? I knew I shouldn't have come. I knew there would be this trapped moment, when all the small talk would run out and we'd have nothing to say.

"So what kind of class was it?" Darlene asks.

"Sorry?"

"Where you met Tarzan. Jim." Just a hint of mocking in her eyes.

"A meditation class."

"TM?"

"No."

"Yoga?"

"No."

"Do you still go?"

"No."

There. So much for that topic. I look around for something to latch onto, a book, a magazine, a plant, anything to talk about.

She says, "I was thinking about having children," and my foot falls off my knee.

"Don't worry," she says, "I'm too old. I'm barren. It's too late." Mock desperation. "Your father wanted nothing to do with it."

"I'm sorry."

"He blamed it on you. He said you'd be too upset, we'd never see you again, it'd be too much." She watches the ash of her cigarette grow for a moment. She looks older than I want her to look. "It was bullshit anyway," she says. "He just wanted to avoid the topic. I let him. I signed up for it."

"I'm sorry."

"I don't even know why I brought it up," she says.

The "boys" come back a little later, red-cheeked and jocular, buddies for life. The trailer shakes when they walk in and Daddy glowers at Darlene when he sees her cigarette.

"Come on there, girls!" he says, clapping his mitts together as if rousing a couple of hens. "Get your jackets on! We're going to go out!"

"Where?" Darlene asks suspiciously.

"It's a perfect day. Conditions could not be better. Let's go!"

"I'm not going golfing," I say.

"Jim-lad has never seen the course," Daddy says. "Come to think of it, neither have you. So let's go!"

"I've seen far too many golf courses with you in my time," I say.

Daddy turns to Jim. "Do you see the kind of battle I've had to put up with all my life? Negativity on all sides. Every brilliant idea squashed. Sand poured into the oil of every pure moment."

"Oh, Daddy!"

"If you won't come with me, come at least with your boyfriend here. Make him feel part of the family."

The word strikes me in a funny way — boyfriend. It doesn't usually apply to me. It makes me feel sixteen with something to hide.

So three of us go. Darlene stays to read a novel, the cover splashed in gold lettering, a ripped bodice, long, shimmering hair. The first tee is on the other side of the inflatable driving range, a slippery walk that takes about ten minutes. Daddy carries the clubs and talks all the way.

"Well, it depends on the bank, of course. Everything depends on the bloody bank. But right now we've got the nine holes and I'm negotiating with Campbell on the other side. With his property we could make eighteen. I've already mapped it out. The greens are most important to me now. That's what people will remember. They'll come up to the first green and say, good God! Look at that! It's the Road Hole! How did it ever get here?"

"The what?" Jim asks.

"Number seventeen at St. Andrews. There's a road that sweeps in behind next to the green, with a stone wall, if you're up against it too bad. But the green itself is kidney-shaped with a big slope, and this deep pot bunker in the middle. You can putt down into it off the green if you're a little bold with your stroke. The Sands of Nakajima. Do you remember that, Garland? Tommy Nakajima trying to get out?"

I shake my head.

"Good God, she forgets her history this one. Brilliant in school but can't remember anything of importance. The British Open 1978. He would've made a run at Nicklaus if he'd only taken par."

Daddy hits first, not even taking time for a practice swing, just a quick swoosh and the red ball — at last the golf people have invented something I can see — sails off into the grey sky, then slides and bounces forever along the ice, right down the middle toward the twisted black branch sticking out of the ground in the distance. Jim takes the club from him, a three-wood, and looks immeasurably awkward addressing the ball. I stand back for safety and he swings like a hockey player, missing the ball and nearly keeling over on the ice.

"Gently! Not so much effort. It's all in the balance," Daddy says.

Jim misses again, does fall this time, ends up at my feet.

"Try it again!" Daddy says.

He just wants to embarrass us — this is what this is all about. He wants to bring Jim into his little sphere of expertise and show him up, make him look foolish, make himself look grand. Look at me! I can hit a golf ball three hundred yards in the middle of winter! It makes me sick. I'm thirty-five years old and here I am back on a frozen patch of ground watching Daddy play his ridiculous games.

Why doesn't Jim just hit the damn ball? But he keeps missing, three, four, five times in a row.

"Hit down on it, son. Don't be afraid to take a bit of a divot. It's only ice. You won't hurt it."

Jim steps back, takes two practice strokes, addresses the ball and fans the air.

"I was hitting it on the range," he says sheepishly.

"You're lifting your head," I say. "And keep your left arm straight. Hit through the ball."

They both look at me with amusement.

"Go on!" I say. "I know what I'm talking about!"

Jim hands me the club, a big smile on his face.

"Well fuck you!" I say, grabbing it from him but talking to Daddy. "You think this is such a hard game. Well it's not. There's a lot more in life that's harder than this stupid game." And I swing — hard — and hit the ball — hard — and it drills down the centre about four feet off the ground and then slides and rolls like it's never going to stop.

"Hey, hey!" Daddy says, twirling me around. We skip Jim's shot this time and start down the fairway, slipping and sliding, Jim carrying the clubs. "Your swing looked so natural," Jim says. "I thought you said you never played."

"But I always knew I could do it!" I say, giddy despite myself. Thank God I didn't miss.

"Look at her," Daddy says, shaking his head.

"What? I'm not supposed to smile?" I say.

"What did I tell you about this feeling?" Daddy asks.

"What?"

"Don't crow about it! For God's sakes, that's the worst thing you can do. A real golfer knows about these things.

When the whole universe is lined up for you, you calm yourself down, take your swing, don't mess it up. And when you turn to watch the ball going perfect, what do you do, jump around? No. You give a little snort. You put your club in the bag. Start walking. Do you know why?"

I look over at Jim, see if he's smiling. "Why?" I ask.

"Because it might happen again. If you don't get dizzy with success. The feeling might just stay. This game isn't about one shot. It's about the whole thing. How you conduct yourself when it's going right and when it's going wrong. That's what it's about."

"He's a philosopher-golfer," I say to Jim.

"I'm serious," Daddy says.

"I know. Thank you," I say, and I kiss him on the cheek, just a quick motion while we're walking.

The two balls are both close to the green, which is white of course, stretching the skin of iced-over snow. I keep looking back to see how far my shot went. From way back there? Impossible!

"You'll probably want to putt it up the slope," Daddy says, dropping a ball for Jim to hit. "Careful of the ridge. And keep your head down."

Jim hits it this time, but too hard. It scurries over the porcelain slickness of the green and bounces right to the back, against the stone wall.

"Probably the best you could do," Daddy says, and does the same thing, but his ball hits the wall a little harder and bounces back onto the putting surface. It creeps, rolls, slides down the slope till finally it ends up in the depression where the bunker must be, under the snow.

I pick up my ball and put it in my pocket, and we all start to laugh at once. "Well I'm not going to do any better than I've already done!" I say. Then Daddy starts down into the bunker but slips and slides, and can't get the ball out, not in three, or four, or five strokes. The ball always slides back to his feet.

"Maybe Darlene had the right idea," Daddy says, giving up and letting Jim pull him out.

"No, let's keep going," I say.

So we walk to the next tee, and I'm struck with a sense of our particular family insanity. I never understood. I probably still don't. But right now this is exactly where I want to be, and I'm doing what I never thought I'd want to do — hit a stupid little ball and feel good about it.

"I don't know if you know about the eighteenth at St. Andrews," Daddy says to Jim. "It's got the widest fairway in the world, you can hit away. But the green has a huge dip at the front, the Valley of Sin. You'll see when we get up to it what I mean." He hits away while he's talking. "My third hole is actually number twelve at Augusta. Garland remembers that one, don't you? Freddy Couples spun back off the green down towards Rae's Creek, and if it hadn't rained so much he would've . . . "

Just his voice, and the dull shine of the day, and Jim here with us. He tries again, pulls it to the left, but this is the biggest fairway, there's no trouble out there. I try not to smile, to gloat, to celebrate. I take my swing and then give a little grunt and start walking, because it might keep happening, you never know, it might just keep on going this way.

TWENTY-SEVEN

By the end of February we're ready for the end of winter, but winter stays long past that, through the long weeks of March, into April, surprising us with the worst storm of the season, masses of warm, heavy snow clogging the streets, spinning our tires, prolonging our sentences. It doesn't seem reasonable to ask Mr. Conners to clear out the farm road one more time when surely it's all going to melt in a day, a few days, by next week at the latest. But it doesn't melt.

The end comes finally, all at once, a blazing brilliant Sunday with everything dripping water and the sky clear as God. (It's the way I used to think of God when I was a little girl; not a white-haired man in the sky but the sky itself, pure and forever.)

I wait till Jim is on the roof before opening the package. From the upstairs bathroom I can hear him shovelling back the remaining snow, the grunt and the push and then the scraping slide, finally the avalanche to the ground.

Everything is very well explained, wrapped in plastic, antiseptic. It's an orderly sort of process. It'll only take ten minutes, once it's all set up.

"I think I've found the problem!" Jim calls, and I lean out the window to talk to him. There's a leak somewhere near the chimney; we've seen the plaster bulges in our bedroom. He clambers down the ladder to get his tools. I lock the door and look at my watch. Six minutes. I listen to the drip of the water outside. It's all around. From off the chimney, down the walls, down the slope, into the stream. Everything's melting. Everything is liquid.

Afterwards, when I know for sure what I already knew, I walk through the house slowly, from room to room, looking at what we've fixed up, what still needs to be done. I'd like to knock out the whole east wall and make a solarium with high arched windows, a rock pool, tropical plants. Somewhere to go in the winter. And I'd like a library upstairs. I don't think we'd need to add anything on but combine two of the junior bedrooms and put in a fireplace, build in the bookcases from the ceiling to the floor. A place to read and listen to classical music, with a window looking over the ridge. I get dizzy just for a moment, sit down, wait for whatever it is to pass. We need more light in here. It's a winter house, but winter's passed now, that time is over.

I pour out two large glasses of lemonade and carry them on a tray out to the ladder, then look up at where Jim is working. He has his shirt off. It's like one of those commercials where you see people skiing on glaciers with their bathing suits on. I start up the ladder, one hand on the tray, the other steadying me rung to rung. I don't know where to look. Down it's too dizzy, up too blue. Like the test paper.

"Careful!" Jim says when he sees me coming up.

"I hate ladders!" I say, stopping to steady myself. It's true — I do hate them. I like my feet on the ground, and I hate the way the aluminum bends when you get halfway up, as if it might fling you off at any moment.

"Keep going!" he says, squatting near the edge. "You're almost there!"

The end is the hardest part, making the transition from the flimsy ladder to the sloped surface of the roof. I hand Jim the tray, try to stay calm. He tries to help me up but I can see myself pulling us both right off, falling twenty feet. I suppose the snow is deep and soft enough. We wouldn't be killed. Only paralysed for life. I wave him off.

He takes the three steps up to the top with insolent skill, sits with his back to the chimney to wait for me. I guess it isn't so hard. I wish my guts weren't seized up like this. I push up onto the roof, feel the ladder move beneath my foot, clutch onto a shingle and hug the black surface, giving a little cry. The ladder stays. Jim nearly spills the drinks trying to get to me. I pull myself up.

"Are you all right?" he asks.

I clamber up, kneel against the V of the roof, clutching the warmth between my thighs. Wait for a moment for my head to clear. It really is sunny up here. And hot. We're both sweating.

He says, "I've been following my repairs book. I'm not sure if this will work, maybe I should wait till everything is completely dry. Inserting shingles is a little tricky. And I should have some roofing tar. Dad used to come home covered in the stuff."

"Do you still want to marry me?" I ask.

"What?"

"You heard me."

"Of course I want to marry you," he says.

"Good," I say, and I close my eyes, feel the sun. God it's been a long time. My heart is just slowing down from the climb. I'm going to have to get down again. I'm going to have to tell him.

"So?" he says, sliding forward, taking my hand.

"I really would like you to take off your pants," I say.

"What?"

"I just want to look at you in the sun."

He puts his cup and the tray on top of the chimney.

"Are we going to do it here?" he asks.

"No. I just want to look at you."

"The underpants too I think," I say.

He does it. Starts to get a little erect, with just my looking at him.

I'm going to have to tell him sometime. I'm going to have to think it through for myself. But for now spring is here and the sky is the colour of God and the sun is too, and the air is hot. I finish my lemonade and take off my clothes and we talk about little things, and then about nothing at all.